SUMMER OF FROST

L.P. Dover

Printed in the United States of America

Summer of Frost
Copyright © 2013 by L. P. Dover
Editor: Melissa Ringsted
Cover Artist: Regina Wamba of Mae I Design
Formatting by JT Formatting

ISBN-13: 978-1490488356
ISBN-10: 1490488359

The Prophecy

Summer, Fall, Winter, Spring
two Courts to Four is what it will bring.
Without the Four the evil will spread,
the Land of the Fae will fall into dread.
The next generation will provide the Four,
the maiden souls and nothing more.
The Power of Four will start with the first,
if he gets the power, only then will you be cursed.
The Power of Four will be drawn to the others,
their power is strong, the power of lovers.
The moment they become one,
only then will the change have begun.
Two Courts to Four is what needs to be,
to save the Land, so shall we see.

Prologue

Sorcha

Tonight was the Winter Solstice Ball, and of course, I was running late ... like always. When I walked through the huge double doors of the ballroom, the force of the exuded power almost knocked me off my feet. I froze in my tracks, darting my gaze around to find the reason for such power. Something wasn't right. Everything around me was normal; the Summer Fae were here, and everyone was dancing around and drinking. Yet, why was my heart pounding out of my chest? Why was the intoxicating energy trying to pull me in another direction?

My date and lover for the time being, Alston, had my arm tightly wrapped around his while we walked through the crowd, acknowledging everyone as we passed. If he felt what I was feeling he wasn't showing it, but how could he not, it was so strong. Alston had short, black hair and striking, blue eyes that reminded me of our Lake of Ice. He walked with a regal gait, so sure and confident, and always had the

Winter Fae women fawning over him. He came from a prominent family of the Winter Court, and was also one of our warriors, even though he could've easily taken a place on the council. He lost the battle when it came time for my Guardian Ceremony, and ever since then, I think he'd secretly held a grudge against Oren, my guardian of two years.

Peering over my shoulder, I glanced quickly at my guardian—who was following close behind—to see if maybe he was feeling what I was. *"Do you feel anything strange, Oren?"* I silently asked him through our connection.

Oren narrowed his eyes and examined our surroundings with great fervor. He replied back, *"I don't sense anything other than your frantic heart. I don't think there's a danger in here. Do you feel threatened?"*

"No, it's not like that," I said, looking around the room. *"I don't know how to explain it, except it's strong."*

"I'll keep a look out," Oren assured me, and gave me a wink.

Giving him a quick nod, I turned my gaze back to the crowd. Alston squeezed my arm, and whispered gruffly in my ear, "I can't wait to get out of here. How about we take a break and head to your room?"

"Is that all you think about?" I hissed impatiently, rolling my eyes. "We just got here."

Alston shrugged, his leer emanating a

mischievous gleam. "I can't help it. You look fucking hot in that dress. Blue is your color, it brings out your …" he said, staring at my breasts, but finished his sentence saying, "… your eyes."

"Somehow, I don't believe that." I laughed, smacking him in the arm.

Normally, I would be all for us leaving the Ball, but the sensation I'd had since coming into the room had given me pause. I was about to tell Alston what I was feeling when my best friend's voice spoke out from behind me, stopping me.

"What are you two whispering about?" Sarette asked, coming to stand before us.

Looking at her was like seeing me in the mirror. From a distance, we looked almost the same with long, straight black hair, same height, and same features. We'd often been mistaken as each other, but if you examined her closely, her eyes were a majestic blue while mine are emerald green, a rarity among my people. No one in the Winter Court had green eyes like me, and mostly everyone thought it had to be because of the prophecy.

I scowled playfully at Sarette, and hooked a finger in Alston's direction. "Your cousin wants to blow off the Ball and have his way with me in my room, or better yet, I have my way with him."

Sarette shook her head, exasperated. "Isn't that the reason you two were late getting here in the first place?"

I nodded. "Yes, and apparently, that isn't enough to satisfy him these days. Maybe I should find someone with fewer needs." I said it as a joke, but in a way I wanted it to strike him where it hurt. Alston got pissed and stalked away, which was my intention with the jab. He was fun to be around, and amazing in bed, but he had started wanting more than I was ready to give.

Sarette followed her cousin's retreating form, but glanced back at me with concern etched on her elegant face. "What's up with you two?"

"I don't know," I remarked, shrugging my shoulders. "He's been really clingy lately, and showing more signs of jealousy and hostility toward Oren. They fight all the time and it drives me insane. I guess he's still angry he lost the battle to be my guardian, but even so, he's gotten really possessive … I don't like it."

A smile took over Sarette's face.

Laughing, she took my hands. "He acts that way because he's in love with you, Sorcha. I know you don't want to be tied down with someone, but he's really taken with you. You should let him in your heart instead of pushing him away. I honestly think you're trying to find reasons to push him away. Wouldn't it be great if we became sisters instead of just best friends? I've never seen him act this crazy over someone … ever."

She was ecstatic when I took her cousin as a

lover. She wanted us to be a family, but if this was how his love was, I didn't want any part of it. I wasn't an expert on affection, but surely it couldn't be smothering like that. Sarette's gaze grew sad, the realization dawning on her that what was about to come out of my mouth wasn't going to be anything reassuring. I couldn't care less about hurting anyone else's feelings, but Sarette *was* like a sister to me, and if I broke things off with Alston it would definitely disappoint her.

Squeezing her hands, I gave her a small smile. "He may love me, Sarette, but I just don't think I can take anymore," I whispered to her. "If he wants to back off a bit and just have fun with me that's fine, but I just don't see him doing that." Immediately, and out of nowhere, I could sense a strong presence behind my back. Sarette's eyes went wide at the same moment I tensed and stood frozen. I cringed, thinking it was probably Alston and he had heard every word I'd said.

My heart began its erratic beating again, and when I slowly turned around to face Alston, I was astounded to see that it wasn't him standing there, but someone else. The man before me was not only lethal and sexy, but he happened to be the Summer Court prince, Drake. His bright, red hair reminded me of the sun on a hot summer day, or better yet, the fire of the dragon inside of him. However, I didn't let his charm sway me. His smoky, gray eyes bore into mine, and when he noticed I didn't melt under his gaze, he tilted his lip up in an arrogant smirk, clearly amused. Cocky bastard.

"Good evening, Princess Sorcha. I don't think we've actually been formally introduced," he expressed regally, bowing slightly. "I'm Drake."

"I know who you are," I replied blandly. "I've heard a lot about you."

He beamed. "Good things, I hope."

"Not really," I teased dryly.

Indeed, I'd heard many things about him. He was an arrogant ass that liked to show off his skills anytime he could, not to mention he probably had a million Summer Fae women lined up to enjoy him in his bed. I didn't know that for certain, but I could only imagine. His life was very secret when it came to women, so needless to say, it drew many speculations. He was ridiculously good looking, and the longer he was in front of me the more I felt a pull to fall into his arms. What the hell was wrong with me?

Laughing, he tilted his head and held out his hand. "How about we dance, and you can tell me all about what you heard. I guarantee most of it isn't true."

I glared at his hand, and then back up to his face, contemplating if I should accept. Before I could take his hand, Alston pushed his way between us, anger emanating off of him in strong waves. "How about you find someone else? Sorcha is with me. I'm sure you'll find another Winter Fae that would be happy to cool your bed."

For a second, I stood there frozen and speechless. In a way, I wanted to see what Drake would do, but I also didn't want to see them fight. It would cause unwanted problems that we didn't need. Slow, and with determination, Drake took a step closer to Alston, standing almost nose to nose with him. "So ... she's with you, huh?"

"That's right," Alston growled.

A wolfish grin spread across Drake's face. He raked his heated gaze down my body quickly, before laying his deadly gray eyes back on Alston. "Keep telling yourself that," he retorted.

Alston clenched his fists, ready to strike, when Drake gracefully backed up and bowed his head slightly at me, never swaying his eyes from mine. "Maybe next time, Princess Sorcha," he murmured, his voice low and seductive.

Out of all my years of always having a smart ass comeback or something witty to throw out, that moment was one of the times I couldn't form words. Alston snaked his arm around my waist, pulling me close, and for that second in time I didn't care. Nothing existed except me and Drake as he backed up slowly, both of our gazes never wavering from each other's. He winked at me before leaving the ballroom, and once he was out of sight, everything immediately returned to normal. My heart beat regularly while everyone came back into focus, and that meant Alston and Sarette's angry glares.

I knew then that everything was going to change after that night. Drake had captured my attention, and I was determined to find out more.

Chapter One

DRAKE

"*Enough!*" I yelled, my voice carrying out over the expanse of the field.

The warriors were on the training grounds battling it out, but they stopped at my command. They bowed before gathering their weapons and clearing the field with haste. They'd been training since sunrise, and I knew they needed their rest. I had to make sure they were ready for when the time came for Ariella's Guardian Ceremony, where they would combat each other for the right to be her guardian.

Light footsteps approached from behind, and I wasn't surprised to see that it was my sister, Ariella, who had taken place by my side. While she searched over the retreating warriors, I could see the mischievous glint in her eyes, and the wheels turning in her head.

"Whatever you have planned, little sister, I can already tell you it won't be wise," I informed her in my most serious tone, even though I knew I was wasting my breath.

She laughed, but I could hear the deceptive tone underneath. "Oh, Drake, when will you get it through that thick dragon skin of yours that I always follow through with my sneaky plans? It's what gives me purpose in life."

I groaned, running my hands through my hair. "That's what I'm afraid of."

Ariella had this way of always making everything difficult for me, and she loved it. Even when I trained her she'd still be stubborn and up to no good, always trying to take me down with her underhanded tactics. She was a good fighter, but never disciplined enough to take it seriously. She always had a dirty trick up her sleeve, and in battle that could be a good thing. Out of all my sisters, she was the most fun to be around. You never knew what you were going to get with her.

Much to my dismay, and never would I say this to them, but I actually missed my sisters, Calista and Meliantha. The palace was a lot quieter with them gone, but it was full of energy when they were here. Meliantha was due any day to have her twins, and once we got the announcement I was sure everyone would be flocking to the Spring Court, maybe even … Sorcha.

Ariella snapped her fingers, trying to get my attention, so I cocked my head in her direction. "Drake, are you okay? You've been acting weird for a while now. You're usually an arrogant ball buster, but I've noticed that you haven't been as hard or mean to the warriors here as of late. What's going on with you?"

Quickly, I averted my eyes from her, and tried to think of an excuse, but none came. Ariella was the last person I wanted to talk to about what was on my mind. Jumping up and down excitedly, she clapped her hands and asked, "Are you seeing someone? That's the only reason I can think of. Who is she?"

Turning my head away from Ariella, I contemplated my next words. What was I to say … that I was in love with a dream? For the past few months, the Winter Court princess had occupied my fantasies every single night. Ever since I met her, she'd taken over every thought in my mind like a plague. I'd even turned down countless nights of bedding the women of our court because all I could see was the Winter beauty inside my head. I couldn't seem to dream of anything else other than her, and what pissed me off about it were the feelings I was having. It was pathetic to be falling in love with a dream, and especially with someone from Winter. Except, if I was honest with myself, I'd say that I was already in too deep, but no one needed to know that.

Smiling, I glanced over at my sister who still had a goofy grin on her face waiting for my lover's name. "I'm sorry to disappoint you, but there's no one. You should know better, Ariella. Love is for idiots who have nothing better to do."

She stared at me in disbelief, but then burst out laughing. "I don't believe you for a second! Say that shit to someone who'll believe you. Drake, I'm sure one of these days you'll find the Summer girl of your dreams. You don't have to hide behind your arrogance, you know. Unfortunately, I'm sure you'd still be the same arrogant ass as always when you do decide to find someone. In a way, I kind of pity the girl that you fall for," she joked. When I growled at her, she smiled and linked her arm with mine. "Oh, calm down, I'm just kidding. Now come and take me for a ride," Ariella demanded. "It's been ages since I've flown with you."

Ariella and I had always had a certain bond. I think it was because she was the youngest of my siblings, and also the one I had to spend a great deal of time with to keep her out of trouble. She happened to be the only one of my sisters who's ridden with me in dragon form. I don't do it often, but when I do I enjoy the times I can be free and fly. Out of the people in my court, I'm the only one who'd been gifted with the ability to turn into a dragon. It made me different, and also lethal. When the final battle with the dark sorcerer comes, I was pretty sure I could handle my own.

However, there were disadvantages of transforming, such as the pain before and the fatigue after. It took a lot of power and strength to be, 'The

Dragon,' but it was a sacrifice I'd happily give to see my sister smile.

"Where would you like to go?" I asked while we made our way to the edge of the field. "We flew over the Spring Court last time, so where will it be this time?"

Ariella smirked in her usual mischievous way, and acknowledged the one place I was hoping she would pick. "I say we fly over Winter this time. Let's give them something to talk about, shall we?"

I smiled, and rubbed my hands together. "Let's go."

I could feel the excitement in my chest as my body prepared for the change. After removing my warrior gear, I knelt down in the soft grass below me. Ariella moved back to give me plenty of space, and folded my clothes into a neat pile. Before I let the dragon forth, I took a few deep breaths to concentrate, in and out. The calmer I was, the less pain my body endured during the change. On the days I was angry, I could shift almost immediately; the pain was explosive, but it was over just as quickly.

The dragon stirred beneath my skin, closer and closer to the surface. My skin stretched and my limbs grew, breaking and snapping while mending quickly back in place as the dragon took over. Gritting my teeth, I slammed my eyes shut. The snaps and cracks of the bones made Ariella gasp, but the sounds were actually worse than what it really was. She saw this every time, and every time she'd do the same thing. The pain was something I'd gotten used to, and I would gladly accept it to get the reward of the freedom it gave me.

My body grew until I soon towered over the trees, and my claws took root into the soft soil below. The fragrance of the land intensified while my sight magnified ten-fold. I could see and hear things over hundreds of yards away, and I could fly to and from each court within a matter of minutes. The fire inside me rumbled in my chest, bursting at the seams to be let out. When the transformation completes, my mind stays the same, and I can think just as clearly in dragon form as I can in my fae form. The ground shook as my heavy weighted claws thumped on the ground as I made my way to my sister.

Ariella climbed up on my back and shivered. "I don't think I'll ever get used to watching you change. The sounds are enough to make me cringe. I can't imagine what it feels like."

I huffed at her, making her laugh. Once she was gripped on tight, I took off into the sky, going higher and higher while my wings carried us swiftly across the land.

I was him … I was 'The Dragon.'.

Chapter Two

Sorcha

"Are you going to tell him?" Oren's words came out as grunts as the rod of my spear landed a hard blow against his ribs. He was trying to distract me, but I knew better than to let him take my mind off of training. He knew I wouldn't falter, but it didn't stop him from trying. We trained every day, and every day he did the same thing to me.

Dodging Oren's blows, in one quick breath I said, "How am I going to tell him, Oren? I haven't seen him since the Winter Ball. I can't just go up to him the next time I see him and say, 'Hey, Drake, you know the dreams you've been having … well, ever since I became a dream walker I had the silly notion to visit you in your dreams, and now I can't seem to stop'."

"I think it would be wise to tell him next time you see him, Princess. You've been taking up the man's dreams for months now. Don't you think the game needs to stop if you aren't going to do anything about it?" Oren stated, piercing me with a glare that challenged me to say otherwise.

I huffed in defeat. "I will … someday, when the time is right."

Whistling, Oren shook his head. "Is that nervous energy I feel coming off of you. Since when do you get nervous? I've never known you to care what others thought."

I kicked him in the shin, and he hissed at the impact. *"I don't care,"* I replied silently with force. *"Now let's stop talking about it and get back to training. I need to get my mind off of it."*

"As you wish, ai dulin."

I wondered what Drake would say when he found out. Our dreams for the past few months have been like nothing I'd ever experienced before in my life. When I turned twenty-one, I had some new abilities come to me. I had always had an affinity for the earth, but now I could dream walk, and I was also a truth seeker. If I wanted to know if someone was telling the truth, all I had to do was touch them and I could sense it. Things worked differently in the dream realm. Drake and I have had several heated moments in our dreams, but in reality it wasn't real. Our interludes were but a taste of the real thing.

Oren took this time to laugh, and I could only assume he saw what I was thinking in my mind. Giving him an evil sneer, I sent him a mental image of what I'd do to him if he so much as breathed a word about it to anyone. I shifted and swayed from his advances while swinging my spear in the process. I landed a quick blow to his backside, and he howled in pain, the smile now gone from his angelic face. His brown eyes were light as caramel, and sensual enough to see the soul beneath them, but he used to not always be like that. He was a swift and deadly killer, and cold as ice to others, but when he won the title of Guardian to me ... things changed. Oren only let me see that certain side of him, just like I only let him see a certain side of me.

In a way, we have no choice since we're bonded, but right now, he looked intent on making me pay for the blows I'd given him. So much for the sweet Oren.

"What are you waiting for?" I taunted him silently. He didn't answer, just kept those brown orbs trained on me. His thick, brown curls didn't even move as he gracefully countered my movements.

The spear was light as I held it in both of my hands, waiting for him to retaliate. We circled each other, mirroring our movements together. The wooden shaft of my spear had been carved and smoothed to perfection, although, I could still feel the ridges of the ancient words engraved underneath my hand. *Groval, poldora, nomin:* Courage, strength, wisdom. For some reason, saying the words made me feel stronger ... faster.

As soon as I repeated the words in my mind, Oren advanced. We parried and sparred for what had to have been hours. I was proud of myself because not once during our hours of training did he get one single hit on me. Oren took training seriously, and he would always push me until he knew I could no longer stand it. Only when exhaustion took over would he let me stop. I dropped to the mat, breathing heavily, while Oren lay down beside me, patting my leg in approval.

"You're getting better, Princess. Your concentration didn't waver a bit, even though I know your thoughts were on a certain prince. I must say that I'm proud of you, ai dulin."

Ever since I was a child he had called me *ai dulin,* which meant, little bird. It was a name that's been stuck with me throughout the years, and it didn't look like he was ever going to stop using it. I actually loved the endearment, since it was the only one I'd ever been given. Oren's past was heartbreaking, and growing up I could always see the hint of sadness in his eyes over his lost love. On the day he was going to ask her to bond with him she disappeared to the mortal realm and never came back. He searched for years and years, but eventually gave up. He had chosen to never be with a woman since then, and had put all of his efforts into being my guardian.

"Thank you," I said, nudging him with my elbow. "I have a wonderful guardian who has trained me well."

Oren looked over at me and smiled. His straight,

white teeth sparkled along with the pale perfections of his skin. He kept watch over me as a child, and it wasn't a shock when he volunteered to battle it out with the other warriors for the title of my Guardian. Oren was over two hundred years old, and had seen things I could only imagine. He didn't look a day over twenty-five, but that's how we all were here. He was the one who carved the shaft of my spear, and engraved the magical words into the wood.

Each princess had taken up a special weapon they were good at maneuvering. Calista had her daggers, Meliantha had her bow, and I had my spear. I had no clue what special weapon Ariella had mastered, or if she was even practicing with weapons. My spear was made from the thistle-birch tree, which made it light and durable. Not only could I use it for throwing, but I could also use it for combat. The tip of my spear was made by the dwarves, and infused with mine and Oren's blood, just like Meliantha had done with her arrows. That way when, or if, I was ever attacked, I'd have my *own* way of defending myself if something were to happen to Oren.

Ever since the incident with Calista and Meliantha, I had been ordered to train. I knew that I was next in the dark sorcerer's plans, so therefore, I had to be ready. Kalen used to help me practice, but now that he was King of the Spring Court, I no longer saw him as much. My training partners were now my guardian, Oren, and my last and only brother of the

Winter Court, Brayden.

Brayden didn't help out nearly as much anymore now that he was the Leader of the Winter Court Army, and spending his time training them. Once Kalen left, the title was given to him.

"I know you miss your brothers, *ai dulin*, I can feel it, but you'll get to see Ryder and Kalen very soon. I'm sure Meliantha will be having those babes any day now, and once she does I'm sure everyone's going to be there. When I say *everyone*, you know who else I speak of, don't you?" Oren asked.

Nodding, I bit my lip. "I knew I would see him when the time came. There's no way he'd miss his niece and nephew being born. He talks about them all the time in the dreams we have, amongst other things. I'm sure he's going to be appalled when he finds out our dreams are real, and that he's let himself open up to me. It didn't start out that way, you know."

Oren grinned. "From what I've seen, you two have grown awfully close the past several months. If what you do in your dreams is real, I'd say he's madly in love with you, and who wouldn't be? You're an amazing woman. I don't think he will be as upset about the dreams as you think he'll be."

I laughed. "Did you miss the part where we argue and fight all the time, Oren? Drake is an obnoxious and arrogant whelp at times, and you know I can never keep my mouth shut when he gets in his moods," I retorted, flustered.

21

"You both have so much in common, but I think it compliments you. He's your flame, and you're his ice. Although, opposite in appearance, you are both similar in spirit. Do you not see where this is headed, *ai dulin*?"

"What do you mean, Oren?" I asked innocently, even though I knew what he was going to say.

"I am saying that I've seen in your mind, and I know what's there. You want me to think that it's nothing between you two when you're actually afraid to fess up to what's really going on. You and Drake have been building a secret relationship for a while now, and the signs are everywhere." When I didn't respond he continued. "He's your other half, Sorcha. When you two see each other again, I wouldn't be shocked if the vision happens when you two touch. Don't tell me you hadn't thought about it."

I groaned and hid my face in my hands. "I'm not going to lie … I have. I felt it when we met, and in our dreams the connection explodes with intense power. We've touched in the dream realm, but I know that doesn't really count since it's only in our minds. I can't imagine what it's going to be like when I see him again."

Oren patted my leg again, and began to sit up. "It'll definitely be interesting, Princess," he admitted.

"What will be interesting?" Alston shouted from the doorway, his harsh voice echoing off the walls. I sat up quickly and groaned at the sight of my past

22

lover's form striding closer. Oren tensed beside me, and leveled a steely glare in Alston's direction, clearly not liking the intrusion.

"I don't think that's any of your concern, Alston. I think it would be wise for you to mind your own business," I snarled while getting to my feet. Oren followed suit and moved to stand beside me, but also to the front of me, protecting. He knew very well of my past with Alston, and how possessive over me he could be. Sarette said it was love, but even I wasn't stupid enough to believe it.

Alston moved forward and made his way to us. His tall, elegant frame was well-muscled and chiseled to perfection. His black hair was in disarray while his armor, still covered in snow, glistened in the lighting of the training room. My brother always had them training outside. Alston's hands were big and strong, and even from across the room, I could see the firm grip he had on the handle of his sword. His piercing blue eyes never left mine as the distance came to a close. I remembered the nights with him very well, and I remember having pleasures with him that I'd never forget.

Once things started to progress with Drake in our dreams, I had let Alston go. When he felt me slipping away from him, he tried to hold onto me more—to keep what we had alive—but I couldn't stay. His eyes used to look at me with longing, but now all I saw when he looked at me was hunger. He thought he could make me come back to him by making me jealous, by parading other women in front of me, but all it did was push me further away. I kept waiting on him to give up on me, but he never did, and I'm starting to think he never will.

Standing before me, Alston rubbed his chin maliciously. "Hmm ... none of my concern? See, that's the thing, my lovely Princess, starting today I'm going to be part of your protection detail. Therefore, I think it pertinent that I know everything that's going on. We wouldn't want anything happening to you, now would we?"

My heart plummeted to the floor, and I clenched my fists in annoyance. I jerked my head over to look at Oren, but he was just as clueless as I was. He shrugged his shoulders, continuing to stare daggers at Alston. "What do you mean you're part of my protection? I don't remember telling anyone I wanted you to be a part of it. In fact, I specifically said I didn't want you a part of it," I snapped.

His slow growing smile looked triumphant. "Yes, I know, but since Sarette is my cousin and I look out for her, I put in a request to be able to protect her when she's with you. She was with me when I asked for it, and completely agrees with me." Gritting my teeth, I stiffened at the thought of my friend betraying me. I was going to kill Sarette for it, too ... or at least kick her ass, whichever one came first. Alston continued, "You have a target on your head, as I'm sure you know, and I'm not going to let my cousin get caught in the crossfire without my protection. Wherever she goes with you, I go." Alston reached up to touch my face, but I smacked it away as hard as I could, making my hand sting with the contact.

He laughed. "I look forward to spending more time with you."

Oren advanced quickly, but Alston backed up and held his hands up in surrender. "No harm, just a love tap. She knows I like them," he taunted, winking at my guardian before smiling at me. Oren's anger was palpable through our bond, but I know he knew very well that I could take care of myself when it came to an old lover.

"The next one won't be just a tap, Alston. I'm sure you remember how you weren't smiling after the last time," I snapped back at him. His smile disappeared, and thankfully, he squelched his next comment and left the training room before things escalated further.

A couple of months ago, he tried one of his many attempts at getting me back. However, all it did was infuriate me, and I ended up giving him two black eyes and a broken nose. Granted, he healed quickly after that, but at least I was able to show him he couldn't dominate me. I know what made it worse was that we were in front of other warriors when I did it; they never let him live it down.

"Is he going to be a problem, *ai dulin*?" Oren

asked.

Aggravated, I sighed. "When is he not a problem?"

I began walking hastily to the door, determination in each step as I made my way out of the palace. I had someone to talk to and it wasn't going to be pretty. My best friend was going to pay for what she did to me.

"I don't like where your thoughts are at. I sense anger, and when you get angry, people get hurt. Where are we going?" Oren demanded, keeping his pace alongside me.

"I have someone I need to talk to, and that someone is going to give me answers, right now!" I exclaimed.

Oren's chuckle could be heard loudly inside my head. *"Let me guess ... Sarette."*

Glaring at Oren, I knew my eyes were ablaze with fire. *"You're damn right."*

Sarette had a lot of explaining to do, and she had better come up with a good reason for doing what she had done. Instead of taking horses, Oren asked if I wouldn't mind walking, thinking it would cool off my nerves the longer it took. Reluctantly, I agreed, knowing very well I tended to do things irrationally when I was pissed.

It didn't take long to arrive at Sarette's dwelling once we headed out of the palace and into the village. She still lived with her family most days, but usually she was with me in the palace. Her parents didn't mind, and neither did mine. They all figured we were safer there anyway, instead of gallivanting out without the protection of the palace walls.

When I tried to knock on the door, Oren stopped my hand from making contact for fear I would knock it down. "Are you serious?" I hissed at him. "I'm not going to beat the door down."

Oren shrugged. "Better safe than sorry, *ai dulin.*"

Rolling my eyes, I stood back while Oren knocked twice on the door and then came to wait by my side. Almost immediately, Sarette answered the door with a genuine smile on her face, but when she saw Oren's expression her gaze quickly landed on me.

"Sorcha, what's wrong?" she asked, concerned. Sarette pushed through the door and grabbed me by the shoulders, searching my eyes for an answer.

Not wanting to waste time, I cut right to it. "Why did you request Alston to be one of your protectors? You do realize we have thousands of other warriors that would kill to watch over you," I replied heatedly.

"How could you do this to me knowing I try to avoid him as much as possible?"

Her shoulders sagged in defeat. "I know you do, Sorcha, but he told me he's trying to change. He came by here earlier and went on and on about you, and I felt bad for him. He really wants you back."

"Bullshit! He may want me back, but I didn't see anywhere in his demeanor earlier that would tell me he's wanting to change. He still seems like the same Alston from before; he's arrogant, demanding, cruel, and manipulative. Do I need to go on?"

Sarette flinched at my words, but I was furious. Her voice was apologetic when she spoke. "I have to believe in him, Sorcha. He's my family, and the closest thing to a brother I have. You of all people should know how important family is. When he tells me he wants to change, I have to believe him. That's what family does."

We stood there staring at each other, waiting for the other to give in. Groaning, I pulled her to me and wrapped my arms around her. I did understand the importance of family, and I couldn't help the fact that one of her closest relatives was a dick. Sarette had never really liked my brother, Brayden, so I guess I could see where she was coming from.

Sighing, I said, "I understand, Sarette, but if he so much as tries to get under my skin I'm going to kick his ass. He knows I can do it, too."

She snickered and squeezed me tighter. "I won't

let him bother you. I don't think he's gotten over the embarrassment of you beating the shit out of him in front of everyone."

"No, I don't believe he has, and neither has anyone else who saw me take the mighty Alston down," I cackled, releasing Sarette from my arms. I may not care for Alston anymore, but he was her family, and that was something that would never change. Unfortunately, I was going to have to grin and bear it.

"Are we okay?" Sarette asked sheepishly. "I don't want you to be mad at me."

I nodded. "Yes, of course we're okay. Now that I've got my anger out I'll leave you be. Will you be by later? I could teach you how to throw a spear, or maybe even get Aric to show you some moves." I waggled my eyebrows when I mentioned Aric's name. Sarette has had a crush on him for ages, and I'd been trying to get them together.

Her eyes went wide and she licked her lips. He happened to be one of the best warriors we had, and the one with the most flattering reputation as well. He was never short on women, but that didn't seem to bother Sarette in the least. I'd be lying if I said I hadn't partaken in a little fun with the warrior myself. He was the one who taught me how to kiss, and even to this day Aric and I still joke about it.

"Can you please keep those thoughts to yourself? I see enough of you and Drake in your mind as it is."

Oren had his arms crossed over his chest with a look of disgust on his face.

Laughing, I turned to him. *"I'm sorry. I'll work on it."*

Sarette saw the exchange and narrowed her eyes. "You better not be talking about me you two."

Oren smiled and sarcastically said, "No, I just got some images in my head of the infamous Aric. Personally, I don't see why you would waste your time with him, but by all means go for it. I just thought you might not want to be known as one of Aric's conquests."

I smacked his arm and gave him one of my 'shut the hell up' looks. Sarette didn't seem to mind, and waved Oren off dismissively. "I would be more than happy to get some moves by Aric. I'll be by later, so tell him to wait for me?"

"Of course!" I grinned, pinning Oren with a steely glare.

Before Sarette was about to close the door, her mouth fell open and she gasped. She lifted her hand and pointed to something off in the distance. "What the hell?" she whispered in awe.

Oren and I both turned around quickly, him grabbing his sword while I grasped my spear thinking there was danger coming, but what we saw in the direction of Sarette's gaze was definitely dangerous, although not to us. Frozen in place, I stared at the majestic sight off in the distance, flying straight toward our court.

"Is that what I think it is?" Oren asked.

My smile grew wider and I nodded. "I do believe so."

Chapter Three

Sorcha

I watched in awe as Drake flew over my court in dragon form. It was amazing, yet terrifying. He was huge, and I found it fascinating how someone my size could change their body to be something of twice the magnitude of an elephant. There were no other creatures in our land with those massive proportions. His reddish and gold dragon skin contrasted greatly with the stark white background of the Winter Court, making him stand out like the magnificent creature he was. It was interesting because his skin was the same color as his hair when he was in his normal form, all red with tints of gold like the setting sun in the Summer Court. Maybe one day I'd be able to see that setting sun.

Drake had told me numerous times in our dreams how he flies with Ariella, and how each time he secretly wished she would choose to fly over the Winter Court. It looked like he finally got his wish. I knew he saw me, because even from high up in the sky I could tell his slit-like pupils were transfixed on me, just like mine were transfixed on him. He circled above a few times before guiding his wings in the direction back to his court. Ariella waved at us from above, and I waved back, secretly jealous that it wasn't me riding up there. I must admit, it had to be fun to be able to fly.

After the spectacle was over, Oren and I headed back to the palace where we separated ways so I could relax for the evening. Night couldn't come soon enough. When it did, I nestled deep within the confines of my bed, falling into a much needed and anticipated sleep, bringing Drake along with me.

I began the dream playing one of Drake's favorite songs on my harp. The setting for our rendezvous was my room in the Winter Palace, and I was sitting on the crimson, velvety seat that sat in the corner by the window. The soft, sensual melody of the song I wrote specially for Drake echoed throughout the expanse of the room. Only Drake, Sarette, and Oren knew of my love for the harp, and in my dreams I could play it freely. It's one of the only things that

relaxed me from the stress of Winter Court life.

The strings thrummed along my fingertips as I played each note, gracefully and with ease. The music was hypnotic as I closed my eyes, soaking in the sounds, and it wasn't long before I was able to lose myself in it. The veil to the dream world began to thin, and I could feel Drake getting closer the more I played. I sensed him behind me, inching closer, until finally his arms enclose my waist.

"Is it bad that I live my life looking forward to the night?" he asked huskily, nuzzling his face in my hair. His hand swept it off my shoulder, and he laid a soft, warm kiss at the nape of my neck. I shuddered as the chills ran down my body.

"No, because I'm the same way," I confessed, moving away from the harp so I could stand in front of him. Taking my face in his hands, he crushed his lips to mine ... wanting and needing. Running my hands through his hair, I tugged him closer, opening my lips further and allowing more of him to enter. His tongue was demanding yet sweet as he feverishly claimed me for his own.

Leaning away from the kiss, I placed my hands on his chest, giving a light push. I'd wanted to tell him for a long time now that these dreams were real, but I knew he wouldn't believe me, not without solid proof. This was just a dream world to him, but I was ready to tell him.

Drake's eyes were full of concern when he

studied me. "Why did you pull away?"

Averting my eyes to the floor, I took a few seconds to think of the questions I wanted to ask him before I looked at him again. "Drake?" I asked.

"Hmm ..." he replied, tucking a strand of hair behind my ear.

"Do you find it odd that you dream about me every night?"

He narrowed his eyes in concentration, and shrugged. "I hadn't really thought about it like that. I guess it is a little strange, but I'm not complaining." He distracted me by dipping his head lower to graze his lips along my jaw and down to my neck. I sighed in contentment, and for a moment I let myself lose all train of thought while Drake ran his hands all over my body, rubbing and caressing.

"You're making it hard for me to think," I chastised him playfully.

"I'm sorry," he whispered in my ear. "It's just ... I've missed you."

I chuckled lightly. "You just saw me last night, but if it makes you feel better, I've missed you, too. What do you want to do tonight? We've travelled all over the world and done everything humanly possible. I guess we need to think of new things to do."

His eyes grew dangerously dark, the gray in them swirling like the mist on stormy seas. He pulled me tighter against his body, his gaze full of want and need, and it didn't take long to figure out where this was going to lead. He bent down, lips almost touching mine, and murmured against them, "I think you know what I want to do."

I bit my lower lip, but he released it by taking it in his mouth and sucking it, hard. I sagged in his arms, knowing my window of opportunity to tell him the truth had just flown away. I was falling way too fast, getting in deeper and deeper. The more we did this, the harder it was not to tell him the truth. How were things going to be when I saw him in person again and told him? We've spent the past ten months getting to know each other in our dreams, but would he see it as a violation into his life, or would he welcome it? I know his wants, needs, and fears, just like he knows mine. There isn't another person in all the Land of the Fae that knows each other better than we know each other. Will things be the same when it's all revealed?

Drake looked down at my dress and smiled. He took a finger and lightly dipped it inside one of the straps, touching my bare skin. It sent chills down my whole body. "You look amazing in blue."

Blue is his favorite color, so obviously, I picked it out for him and he knew it. I could tell by the sly smile on his face when he mentioned it. Drake pulled the straps of my gown down off my shoulders, and lightly tugged it to where it settled below my bare breasts. My chest heaved up and down with my erratic breathing while his touches left me aching for more.

He circled his thumb over my nipple and smiled when I moaned under his touch.

"Drake, there's something I need to tell you," I whispered.

"What is it, beautiful?" he asked.

I was trying to think clearly, but when he trailed his tongue down my neck and to the mound of my breast, I lost all train of thought. Getting on his knees, he cupped my ass and pulled me to him so my full and heavy breasts were right in front of him. My fingers tangled in his hair as he licked and sucked on my nipple, biting every now and again. If it weren't for him holding me up, I would've crumbled to the floor.

Drake left my breast and kissed a path down my stomach, sliding my dress down with him until it pooled on the floor. "You're so beautiful," he murmured softly.

Panting and heated to the core, I grew weak at his words. Even his voice turned me on. He stood again, and as determined as I was, I began to remove his clothes, not wanting to wait any longer. His shirt and pants were gone in the blink of an eye, and he was standing before me, naked and hard as a rock.

The expression on his face was smoldering as he looked up and down my body. Still standing, he cupped me gently, rubbing against my core, before slowly entering his fingers into my slick, wet heat. Gripping him tightly, we both moaned together

37

feverishly while I moved against his hand. He worked his fingers faster, and I screamed out with my orgasm, not caring how loud I was. We were alone, just me and him, in our dream world.

Drake lifted me in his arms and carried me to the bed, laying me down gently. "Did that feel good?" he asked, grinning triumphantly.

"Amazing," I admitted wholeheartedly, breathing hard and shuddering from the orgasm.

He climbed up on the bed and pushed my legs apart with his knee, settling his weight lightly upon me. I moaned in anticipation when I felt the hardness of his cock pressed against my leg. "What is it you needed to tell me?" Drake asked softly.

He leaned down and kissed me gently, and opened my mouth further by sliding in his tongue. His taste was too intoxicating, too demanding. How could I answer anything when I could barely think? All I wanted was him, here ... now ... always.

Breaking away from the kiss, I answered with a lie, "It's not important. I can tell you later. All I want is you, and nothing else."

He stared at me for a second, doubting, and when I smiled at him reassuringly he brushed it off and continued the slow torture of my body. "Are you ready?"

To answer his question, I frantically bestowed bruising kisses upon his lips, hoping he would get the picture. He growled low in my ear, and with one gentle thrust he entered me fully. Arching off the bed, I grabbed his shoulders and wrapped my legs around his waist. We had fooled around in our dreams, but we'd never gotten this far. There were many times when we came close, but it never felt right until now. No matter what happened after this, he needed to know the truth. I had to tell him.

"Are you okay? I'm not hurting you, am I?" he asked hesitantly.

I smiled. "I'm more than okay, and it feels amazing."

Moving my hips in tune with his, we settled on a rhythm; deep and slow, yet raging with passion. His cock pulsed inside my body, letting me know he was close. Gripping him tighter with my legs, I moved my hips faster, spurring on my own orgasm to explode.

"Fucking hell ... Sorcha! I'm going to come."

"Keep going," I urged him.

My orgasm was close, and the moment it exploded through my body I arched off the bed, raking my nails down Drake's back as he gripped me tighter, releasing his own pleasures inside my body. Drake collapsed on top of me, breathing hard and still heavy between my legs. He kissed me on the lips, and I could taste the salty dew of his sweat, reminding me how hard he worked to pleasure my body.

"You are amazing!" he told me, taking his hands and placing them on the sides of my face.

"So are you," I answered back breathlessly.

He stared at me for a few minutes, and when he finally opened his mouth to speak, he slowly began to disappear. Dammit! He couldn't go now, not yet!

"Sorcha, I ..."

He faded away before he was able to tell me the rest. In my heart I knew what he was going to say, or at least what I hoped he was going to say, but in my head it was screaming that I'd gotten in too deep. What had I done?

Chapter Four

DRAKE

I bolted out of the dream when a loud knock came from someone at my bedroom door. Groaning, I got out of bed and stomped to the door, determined to kill whoever it was that interrupted what had to be the most amazing dream.

"This better be good!" I yelled, opening the door.

The person who greeted me was none other than my pain in the ass sister, Ariella, with the biggest smirk on her face. "My, my … look who got up on the wrong side of the bed," she teased.

"What do you want?" I grumbled, turning away and heading back to the bed. Collapsing on top, I took a deep breath. There was no way I was going to be able to get back to the dream.

"You need to get dressed. We're going to the Spring Court," she called out impatiently, throwing a bundle of clothes at me.

Lifting my head, I spied her rummaging through my drawers and putting clothes into my satchel. "Have the little ones come yet?" I asked.

"Almost!" Ariella exclaimed, waving her hands in the air. "I want to get there before they do! Now hurry up! I have your clothes packed."

Once Ariella left, I sat there thinking about everything that was happening. This was going to be my chance to see Sorcha! She had to be there, I just knew it. I got dressed quickly and had a group of warriors prepped and ready to go in a matter of minutes. We would arrive at the Spring Court no later than that afternoon.

When we passed through the Spring Court gates, Ariella galloped the rest of the way to the front of the palace, where she abandoned her horse and scurried inside. Ashur, Meliantha's guardian, was standing on the steps and came to greet me.

"It's a pleasure to see you, Your Highness," Ashur acknowledged, bowing slightly.

"Same to you," I replied. "Are we in time? Ariella *had* to make sure she got here before the twins came."

Ashur laughed. "You were almost too late. She's actually having them now." His brows furrowed, and he winced. "As a matter of fact, Meliantha is doing her best to shield her pain, but she's not really doing it so well. I thank the heavens every day that I'm not a woman."

I nodded in agreement. "You and me both, Guardian."

Ashur guided me into the palace and through several corridors. I was expecting to hear screams of pain, but as I approached the room all I could hear were screams of joy. Ryder was standing outside the door when I sidled up. "Couldn't handle it in there?" I joked.

Ryder turned around and laughed. "Once the babies started coming I hightailed it out of there. I'm sure Kalen was fine without the moral support."

"I bet his pansy ass fainted." I laughed.

Ryder clapped his hand on my shoulder. "Just wait until it happens to you, my friend."

At that moment, Ariella burst out of the room laughing and crying. She ran up to me and pulled me by the arm and into the room while Ryder followed. Everyone was smiling as they looked upon the two little babes wrapped in blankets. Elvena cleared away all the bloody linens and smiled at me before leaving the room. My twin sister, Calista, was being the mother hen, as always, dabbing a washcloth over Meliantha's forehead and helping her to drink a cup of water.

Kalen was sitting on the bed, staring at the

bundle in his arms in awe. Meliantha smiled over at him, but when her gaze found mine she called me over, beckoning me excitedly. "Drake! You have to see this," she said jubilantly.

When I walked over and glimpsed the babe in her arms, I couldn't help but beam at what I saw. "Red hair," I sighed.

Meliantha grinned. "Just like us. His name is Kale, and your niece's name is Lia."

"Beautiful names, sister," I whispered, leaning down to kiss her on the cheek.

Calista took this time and stood up to give me a hug. "Dad is going to be thrilled to know his red hair was passed down." She laughed. "Are Mom and Dad coming?"

I nodded. "They'll be here tomorrow. Ariella was in too much of a hurry to wait on them," I said, shooting Ariella an exasperated glare.

Ariella shrugged noncommittally. "Sorry, you all know I'm not very patient."

"That's for damn sure," Calista agreed with a smile on her face.

Calista and Ariella bantered back and forth, making everyone laugh, but there was another matter that was eating away inside me. Impatient as I was, I had to know if Sorcha was going to make an appearance. Sounding as non-interested as I could, I directed my question to Kalen. "Is your family coming?" I asked him.

Kalen smiled at his daughter before answering me. "Oh yes, they're coming. Calista sent Nixie out there to tell them this morning, but only Brayden and Sorcha are able to come early."

My heart did a triple beat and I had to stop myself from smiling. I looked around the room quickly to make sure no one heard it or saw my traitorous smile, but I was too late. Meliantha smiled at me and tilted her head inquisitively. *Shit!* I thought to myself. I should've known I could never get away with anything when she was around.

"Would you like to hold your nephew?" Meliantha asked, letting her real question slide.

Sweat broke out in my palms, and my eyes went wide. I had never in my life ever held a baby, and I balked at the thought that I would do something wrong. "I don't want to hurt him," I admitted sheepishly. "What if I drop him?"

"Nonsense!" my sister answered. "You're not going to drop him."

Calista took Kale from Meliantha and placed him gently in my arms. It felt awkward at first, and honestly, I didn't know what to do. I was scared to move or breathe for fear that I would do something wrong, so I stood there frozen in place. After a few minutes, I was starting to get the hang of it. I walked around the room, cuddling the baby in my arms, and watched as he slept with his little thumb in his mouth.

Out of nowhere my heart began to pick up speed

and that pull I felt long ago at the Ball came back full force. It was when the dark-haired beauty entered the room that I realized it was coming from her. Her eyes found mine and we both came to a complete halt.

Chapter Five

Sorcha

When I walked into the room, I wasn't expecting to see Drake cooing and smiling at the baby in his arms. My knees felt weak in that moment and I would have toppled over if Brayden wasn't beside me. It was a beautiful sight before me, and I couldn't stop the smile from forming on my lips if I tried. We stared at each other for a long-lasting few seconds, but then Drake turned his face away in what I assumed was embarrassment.

His skin turned red, and I could tell he was gritting his teeth. I didn't know what I was expecting, but I had to keep reminding myself that he had no clue about our dreams being real. To him, he only met me at the Winter Ball and that was it. After the last dream we had, I guess I just expected more.

The air in the room had turned electric, the tension flowing like waves all around us. Not only did Drake and I have a stare off, but I also noticed out of the corner of my eye, that Brayden and Ariella were doing the same thing, too. Silence filled the room, making it uncomfortable, so I decided to break away from it all and go to my brother.

Kalen was on the bed beside Meliantha so I rushed over and knelt by his side. "Congratulations," I whispered to him and Meliantha so I wouldn't wake the sleeping child in Kalen's arms. Brayden clapped Kalen on the shoulder and congratulated him as well.

"Thank you for coming," Kalen said, kissing me on the cheek, and nodding to Brayden.

"Anytime," I replied.

Meliantha held out her arms, so I went to her side of the bed and hugged her gently. "It's nice to see you again, Sorcha."

"It's nice to see you, too," I told her. When I pulled back, she gave me a knowing smile while looking back and forth between me and Drake. I cleared my throat and shifted uncomfortably by her side. *Was I that easy to see through?* I thought to myself. I looked back at Drake and he averted his eyes so quickly I had no clue if he was even looking at me or something else.

"Would you like to hold Lia?" Kalen asked, catching my attention.

"No!" I exclaimed, a little too loudly, clearly sounding nervous.

Kalen laughed and walked over to me, placing the baby in my arms even though I was shaking like a leaf. "Drake acted the same way, but look at him," he said, peering over at Drake, who was acting fidgety and uptight now that the attention was on him. "He's an expert now. You'll be fine, and besides, I'm sure you'll have your own children someday, so it's good to have the practice."

"I don't think so, dear brother. I'm not the motherly type."

He scoffed and shook his head, but when he settled back on the bed beside Meliantha I heard him whisper, "She'll change her mind." I chose to ignore his comment by giving my attention to the little one I was holding.

I did wonder what it would be like to have one of my own, but I also knew I had plenty of time. There were still so many things I wanted to do and see before I had a family of my own. Out of the corner of my eye, I could see Drake staring at me, but I didn't acknowledge him. I didn't want to give anything away in that room with everyone watching, especially when it killed me not to return his gaze.

We all left the room to give Meliantha and Kalen some alone time with the babies and for them to get some rest. When we arrived we were shown to a set of rooms where Alston and Sarette had decided to stay while I visited with my family. I left without speaking to Drake, even though he looked like he wanted to speak to me. I thought I was ready to tell him … but I wasn't. Oren was going to scold me, I was sure of it.

Meliantha and Kalen insisted we stay for the night so Brayden and I had agreed, even though I knew Brayden didn't want to. His home was in the Winter Court and he loathed having to get accustomed to a new court. On the way to my room, I overheard one of the servant's mention that the Summer Fae were staying as well. I knew that would give me more time to work up the nerve to tell Drake about what had been going on. *Maybe I could break it to him in our dreams,* I thought to myself.

When I opened the door to my room, I silently groaned at the sight of Alston sitting on my bed. "How are your family and the babies doing?" he asked.

"Like you care," I hissed, heading to the window and taking off my gear in the process. Gazing out at the landscape, I noticed for the first time how beautiful it was with colorful flowers as far as the eye could see. Kalen's pack of wolves were frolicking and chasing each other across the land, and it made me smile. I missed his wolves being at the Winter Court. I could picture myself living there amongst the milder temperatures and the smells of Spring, but it wouldn't do well with my cold blood.

Alston came up behind me, closing the distance to where I could feel his body lightly touching mine. What the hell did he think he was doing? "I do care," he whispered in my ear. "Anything that involves you is something I care about."

"You're full of shit," I argued, moving closer to the window to get some distance.

He placed his hands gently on my shoulders and turned me around. I was shocked with how gentle he was being, but I was sure it was just a farce. However, his eyes had lost the coldness to them, which caught me off guard. "When are you going to realize that I'm honestly trying to change? You fell for me once and I know you can do it again."

"It's not that simple," I said.

His lip curled up in the corner in a half-smile. "Nothing is ever simple." He paused to look out the window before coming back down to me, his icy blue eyes looking soft and genuine for once. I hadn't seen that side of him in a long time, and I can honestly say I missed it. He was my friend long before he became my lover.

"What's changed, Alston? Why are you being like this now?"

He shrugged. "I didn't realize how pushy I was being until Sarette and I talked. She pretty much threatened me and said I was screwing up all chances for us to be together. I can't let that happen."

"People don't just change overnight," I uttered, skeptical of his intentions.

Alston took my hands, and against my better judgment I let him kiss my palms. "I know that, but I'm going to work really hard. Just give me a chance."

Oh, how I wished it was Drake in front of me professing his love instead of Alston. Alston let go of my hands and tilted my chin up with his finger so I could meet his eyes. "How about we go for a walk? It's not every day we get to come to the Spring Court, and I know you like it here. I could see it in your eyes."

In a way I wanted to be alone, but a walk through the gardens would probably help my sour mood. "Okay, but I want Sarette to come with us," I insisted, knowing that probably spoiled his plan to seduce me, but he surprised me by smiling and nodding his head. *Maybe he was serious about changing,* I thought to myself, but I knew better than to fully believe it.

"I'll go fetch her," he agreed after kissing my cheek.

After Alston left the room, it gave me a few minutes to myself. I sat by the window on the plush window seat and opened it, letting in the rosy Spring air. I breathed it in deeply before calling out silently to my guardian. *"Oren, where are you?"*

"Right next door, ai dulin, listening to you and

Alston."

"Stalker much?" I laughed, earning a laugh from him in return.

"Sorry, but I kind of have to be. Just be careful with Alston when you're by yourself," he chided, worry eminent in his voice.

"Sarette will be with us, and I know you'll be close by. You know I can take care of myself. I've done it before, and I honestly think he's serious about trying to change. He seems ... different somehow."

Oren sighed. *"I still don't like him. Anyway, you need to find Drake and tell him what's going on."*

"I will, Oren," I huffed impatiently. *"When the time is right I will."*

"Good, now go on your walk and try not to fall into Alston's clutches again."

"You have nothing to worry about," I assured him.

I closed our connection so I could think without knowing Oren could hear me. If Drake was the one for me then why wasn't he coming to me like Ryder did with Calista, and the way Kalen did with Meliantha? *Was it because we were both hard-headed as hell?* I wondered. One of us was going to have to suck it up and make the first move, and it was looking like it was going to be me.

Chapter Six

DRAKE

After everyone had scattered to do their own thing, I was tempted to follow Sorcha and talk to her. *What was I going to talk to her about?* I asked myself. She would think I was crazy if I started talking to her like I did in our dreams. She'd laugh in my face if I told her what we did every night in them together. My feet moved of their own accord, and guided me toward the pull that I knew was her.

"Fuck it!" I groaned out loud, making my decision. "I need to suck it up and find her."

I ran into a servant along the way and she happily pointed me in the direction of where Sorcha would be staying. My heart thumped heavily in my chest the closer I got, the same way it felt when I got close to her at the Winter Ball. I was going to talk to her and go from there. Everything was going to be fine ... or so I thought. However, my excitement died in its tracks when I turned the corner and saw someone I really didn't want to see. *What the hell was he doing here? Surely Sorcha wasn't still with him?* I wondered.

"Ah, Prince Dragon, so nice to see you again," Alston sneered sarcastically.

He narrowed his eyes at me and took up a defensive stance. His hackles were raised, which clearly let me know he wasn't as calm as he wanted me to believe he was. After our confrontation at the Winter Ball, I made sure to find out all about Sorcha's lover. Apparently, he came from a wealthy family and was also the cousin to Sorcha's best friend, Sarette. I was hoping that would explain why he was there.

"I wish I could say the same," I retorted back.

Alston smiled at my comeback, but it quickly disappeared. "Are you here to see Sorcha? Because we were just getting ready to go for a walk. I'd ask you to join us, but I really don't want to."

Feigning boredom, I answered, hoping my lie was believable, "Frankly, I would rather stab myself in the eye before having to spend any more time around you. If you must know, no, I'm not here to see Sorcha, but I am shocked to see you here. I thought she would've come to her senses by now."

Alston grinned and winked at me. "Sorry to disappoint you, but we're still going strong … if you know what I mean."

He was goading me, but I knew I couldn't act on my anger and give him the satisfaction. "Glad to hear it," I lied, balling my hands into tight fists. I had to get away from him before the rage got the better of me and I looked like a jackass. Turning on my heels, I headed back the way I came. "Have fun on your walk," I grumbled over my shoulder.

"Oh, I will," Alston called out, taunting me with the double meaning in his tone.

Picking up my pace, I sped out of the palace, losing my clothes in the process and not caring who saw. I needed the release, and I needed to clear my head. *How and when did I start feeling like I couldn't stay in control?* I asked myself.

The fury in me fueled the dragon, and I gave in to it. My body stretched and my bones broke with the change as I ran toward nothing in particular. I just ran, trying to get the aggression out, and trying to get the Winter princess out of my mind as well. The transformation happened almost instantly, and with one flap of my wings I was in the sky where nothing and no one could bother me.

After spending hours in the dark, cool sky, I had finally decided to come down once my mood settled.

The ground was wet and soft as I collapsed, naked and fatigued upon it. Falling asleep in the open wasn't a going to be a good idea, so I used the energy I had left and walked back to the palace. The warriors posted outside didn't say a word as I walked past them. The clothes I shed earlier were lying in a heap on the palace steps, and I was pretty sure Ariella was probably the one who did that for me.

Pulling them on quickly, I headed inside, going straight to the room that was given to me for the evening. Once I fell onto the bed and closed my eyes, it didn't take long for the familiar pull to drag me under.

The setting of the dream this time was the Spring Court in one of the many gardens around the palace. Sorcha had her back to me, but she was pacing back and forth in the small gazebo up ahead. These dreams were beginning to get ridiculous, and in a way I wished they would stop. Leave it to me to dream about someone I couldn't have, or better yet, someone that didn't even exist.

The Sorcha in my dreams was kind, loving, fun, strong, yet very stubborn, and so full of life and excitement. We fought a lot, but it was always fun as hell. I like a woman who can keep me on my toes, and this Sorcha could do it. It was starting to get pathetic how I've made her up in my dreams.

The one thing that pissed me off was that the real

Sorcha had to be a shallow bitch if she considered Alston to be someone worth being with. I came to the conclusion that these dreams needed to stop, and they were going to now. I couldn't waste my time on a fantasy anymore.

When Sorcha heard me coming, she turned around and gave me a slow growing smile. It was the same smile she gave me after I made love to her. I hesitated for a second, thinking there was no way I could let her go, but then reality hit me again that this was only in my imagination. Maybe I needed to find someone to fill my bed, surely that would help get these damn dreams out of my head and clear my thoughts.

"Drake!" she called out excitedly, beaming.

When I didn't respond, she slowed her approach and eyed me wearily. "What's wrong?"

"What's wrong?" I repeated. "I want the dreams to stop, that's what's wrong."

She flinched as if I'd hit her, and backed up a step, looking confused. "I don't understand. After last night I thought things were going perfectly. You made love to me, Drake. Are you saying that didn't mean anything to you?"

"That's the thing, Sorcha," I replied, closing the distance. Taking her by the shoulder, I looked deep into her eyes, and balked at the hurt displayed in them. I couldn't get over how they're the same emerald green as the real Sorcha's, and just as

beautiful. Exasperated, I motioned my arms to our surroundings. "All of this isn't real, none of it is. You're just a figment of what I've imagined the real Sorcha to be like. You're not her, and I want all of this to stop. I've never been this hard up over a girl before, and I'm not going to start now. It has to end; even if I never go to sleep again, I have to get you out of my head."

"You don't understand," she said quickly, grabbing me by both arms with bruising force. "You have to let me explain."

Pulling away from her grasp, I moved away slowly. "There's nothing to explain. I want them to stop ... now."

"You're not even going to hear me out?" she yelled.

Turning my back on her, I began walking away. "No!" I exclaimed over my shoulder. I could hear the wood split after she punched one of the gazebo posts, and I was thankful that it wasn't my face she'd hit. Sorcha knew how to fight, and with her spear, she made a volatile opponent. I had fun training her in my dreams, but now it was going to be all over. I was going to be free.

"Fine! You want them to stop? Wake up you arrogant jackass!"

My eyes flew open instantly with Sorcha's last words echoing through my mind. I got what I wanted, but why did I feel so bad? The room was dark, signaling that morning had yet to come, but I could feel it steadily creeping closer. I was hesitant when I closed my eyes again, thinking my dream would pick up where it left off, but I was surprised how empty I felt when all that went through my dream was nothing except darkness.

Chapter Seven

Sorcha

"Everyone's ready to go, *ai dulin*," Oren insisted after opening the door to my room. "Are you ready?"

"Just about," I answered. "I just need to finish this letter." Taking in a deep, frustrated breath, I scribbled out the last few lines, signing my name at the bottom.

"Why do I get the feeling that you're mad about something?"

"It's because I am, Oren. Drake wouldn't hear me out when I tried to tell him about our dreams, so I'm letting it all out in the letter. One way or another he's going to hear me out. It took all I had not to chase after him and beat the shit out of him for walking away from me."

Oren chuckled and came over to take a peek at the angry words scribbled on the parchment. His eyes went wide and he whistled. "I don't think this is the way to tell him, nor do I think you doing it in your dream was the way either. Give him the letter if you want, but I think it'd be a big mistake. He may have been a dick last night, but you need to think about it from his standpoint before you run off saying things you'd regret."

I huffed. "Fine! I'll speak to him before we leave. How did you learn to be so calm about things?"

Oren tilted his lip in a half-smile. "It took years and years of practice, Princess. Finish up and I'll meet you out front," he said softly.

"Okay, just give me a few minutes to say my good-byes."

First, I needed to tell Kalen and Meliantha farewell, and then find Drake to get everything out in the open. Rolling up the letter, I secured it with a tiny blue ribbon, and placed it inside the small pouch on my belt that was connected to my armor. Now that I'd been trained in combat, I always wore my warrior gear when I travelled, Brayden's orders. It wasn't very comfortable, but it sure as hell would protect me from unwanted arrows flying through the air or a swipe of a sword. Grabbing my spear, I attached it to the harness on my back and headed for the door. The palace was quiet as I made my way through the corridors, breathing in the delicious aromas of roses that were in vases lined up and down the hallways.

When I reached Kalen and Meliantha's room, I knocked lightly on the door, hoping I wouldn't wake the little ones if they were asleep. Kalen answered the door carrying his wide-awake little boy in his arms.

Kale's bright red hair reminded me so much of Drake, but the eyes …

"What the …" I started, staring in awe at my nephew and then back up to Kalen. "He has purple eyes," I whispered, eyes wide open in surprise.

Kalen smiled, but Meliantha was the one who spoke. "They both do," she announced, elated.

I trailed past Kalen to Meliantha's side where sure enough my niece, Lia, had purple eyes as well. "This is amazing," I murmured, not taking my eyes off the little girl. "I guess you're not the only one now."

Meliantha laughed. "No, and thank the heavens for that. I was tired of being the only one. Hopefully, when these two get older and have children of their own, there will be more faeries with amethyst eyes."

"I sure hope so. I know what it's like to be the odd one out."

It didn't bother me to be the odd one out. I kind of liked being my own person and not blending in with the norm. No one has ever had green eyes in the Winter Court, and most of the time my people just overlooked it. They all knew it had to be because of the Prophecy and me being one of the Four.

"I'm sure when you have kids one of them will have your beautiful green eyes," Meliantha added, looking thoughtful.

Shrugging noncommittally, I turned to my brother. "Yeah, kids are nowhere near in my future. I just wanted to come by and say farewell, and to say thank you for letting me visit."

Kalen came up to me and kissed me on the cheek. "Anytime. It was great seeing you. I've missed giving you hell," he teased.

I laughed. "I've missed you, too. Things just aren't the same with you and Ryder gone. Brayden is about as fun as an ice shard stuck up the ass."

Kalen doubled over laughing. "I am definitely going to tell him that! What's bad is that you're right. Hopefully, one of these days he'll open up and have some fun. Goodness knows Ryder and I've tried to get him to loosen up." He paused and wiped the tears from under his eyes. "I do hope you come back to see us soon. Mel and I would both love to have you. It would definitely keep things interesting around here."

"I'll keep that in mind." I smiled at them both, and kissed the little ones, before leaving their room. Now it was time to suck it up and find Drake.

After searching through the palace, and knocking on the door to the room he stayed in, I was met with silence. *Where was everyone?* I wondered. When I walked out of the palace, our Winter warriors were on their horses ready to go, except Sarette. She and Ariella were on the steps, talking.

"Hey," I said, catching their attention while descending the steps.

"It's about time," Sarette teased. "I was starting to think you wanted to stay here."

"No," I expressed quickly, shaking my head. "I just wanted to say bye to my brother and Meliantha."

Someone whistling caught my attention from behind me, and I turned to see that it was Brayden riding up on his horse. "Sorcha, are you ready to go? We need to get going!" he called out. He gave me an impatient glare, but then his gaze lingered on Ariella just a tad bit longer than normal.

Out of the corner of my eye I could see Ariella pretending not to notice. When I faced her, she cleared her throat and bowed her head, averting her eyes. "Be safe going back home, Sorcha."

When she lifted her head, I narrowed my eyes at her, but all she did was smile innocently. She wasn't fooling me. "I'll be safe. I always am," I drawled out. "When are you going back to Summer?" I really wanted to know where Drake was, but I didn't want to ask outright.

Ariella grinned excitedly. "I'm actually staying here for a few more days. I'll be travelling back with my parents once they come and leave. Not only do I get to spend more time with the babies, but there are a lot of handsome warriors here that I'd like to get to know."

I loved her flippant attitude, and found myself smiling at her flirtatiousness. Ariella was not a bashful female by any means, and if she ever came to the Winter Court again I was sure she'd give my warriors something to talk about, maybe even my brother, Brayden.

Changing the subject, I casually asked, "What about Drake? When is he leaving?"

"Oh, he already left not too long ago. I don't know why he was in such a hurry," she admitted curiously. "He just said he had to leave and didn't want to be here anymore."

My heart felt like it sunk in my chest, and was about to explode. He didn't want me in his dreams, and now he was gone. How was I going to talk to him?

"I'm sure he had his reasons," I replied smoothly. "Take care, Ariella. Hopefully, we'll see each other again soon."

She nodded her head and smiled. Oren and Alston were both waiting by my horse when I approached. Once I settled onto my horse, Alston winked and patted my leg, but I just couldn't bring myself to smile. Too many emotions were warring in my body, and I had no clue how to feel. Mainly I was angry, but mostly at myself if I was being honest.

"Are you going to be okay?" Oren asked silently.

Taking a deep breath, I sat up straighter on my horse. *"Of course, Oren,"* I replied, keeping my face devoid of the turmoil going on inside my body. When I glanced his way, his raised eyebrows and pursed lips informed me he didn't believe my lie for a second. Hell, I would've done anything to believe it.

"I can't wait to get home," Sarette sighed, riding beside me.

"Me too," I mumbled. "But it was great seeing my brother and his family."

Sarette was on my left side while Alston was on my right, riding close to me. Oren trailed behind me, keeping his ever watchful eye on the forest surrounding us. He looked preoccupied with something, but before I could ask, Alston began to speak.

"Do you mind if we talk tonight?" Alston asked, sneaking a glance back at Oren before whispering, "Alone."

Immediately, I glanced at Sarette, who of course had a smile on her face and a twinkle in her eye. I silently groaned and bit my cheek before turning back to Alston.

"That'll be fine," I answered him with faux enthusiasm. "Just give me some time to get settled, and then I'm all yours."

The smile he gave me was alluring and sexy, and I tried to ignore the hidden meaning behind it. He was going to try and lure himself back into my bed, but I wasn't falling for it. In a way, I wanted to release my frustration by doing something foolish like that without my heart getting in the way, but I knew it wouldn't let me. Or at least I hoped it wouldn't let me do anything foolish.

My wayward thoughts were put on hold when Oren spoke in my mind. *"Sorcha, something's not right."* Instantly, I jerked my head in his direction. I could feel his concern and worry floating across the bond ... danger was coming, and it was coming fast.

At that moment, I could see Brayden up front, circling around and headed straight for me. When he approached, he looked dangerous and in full control. His demanding words were directed to me and Sarette. "I want you both to back up and take cover. If we begin to lose ground I want you to run as fast as you can back to the Spring Court and get help. Whatever happens, I don't want you trying to help. I need you two to run, do you understand?"

"No!" I hissed, reaching for my spear. "I've been training for years, and I know how to fight. The dark sorcerer is going to find me no matter what we do. Pretending otherwise is just being naïve. You can't make me run, Brayden. I might as well fight my way through it."

"Me too," Sarette snapped, pulling out her sword. "If you haven't noticed, Sorcha and I aren't little girls anymore. We're ready to do this!"

I smiled at my friend and she smiled back

triumphantly, knowing Brayden wouldn't want to waste his breath in arguing. Infuriated with me, Brayden snarled and was about to yell at me, but he didn't get the chance because out of nowhere the evil began to strike. The dark sorcerer's army was coming straight for us.

"Attack!" Brayden yelled, drawing his sword.

The earth below me trembled with the footsteps of the mighty army coming toward us. We were outnumbered, but it didn't stop us from fighting. Swords clashed as the army made contact with ours. Magic permeated the air, but I was ready, ready to fight.

"Stay close to me, *ai dulin,*" Oren growled.

"I will!"

Alston bounded off into the fight, drawing a scream from Sarette who wanted him close to her. I lost sight of him in the fray. Momentarily I was shocked; all I could focus on were the traitors of my land coming for blood with their eyes fixed on me and Sarette. My friend appeared ready and hungry for a fight.

"Get ready, Sarette!"

She gave me an evil grin. "Oh, I am! These idiots will regret the day they messed with the two baddest bitches of the Winter Court!"

We both smiled at each other before taking off screaming, and wielding our weapons at the enemy. I'd never killed anyone, but I'd do anything necessary to protect my people. With my spear in hand, I fought. Using my earth abilities, I trapped the enemy in the earth and impaled them one by one with my spear.

My first kill was an elf, and the moment I thrust my spear through his heart I could've sworn I saw a smile pass over his face. He wanted to die. My gut clenched with the thought that some of them might've been forced to do this, to turn traitor to their people, but there was nothing I could do about it at that moment except protect my people.

When the army began losing numbers, more would come to take their place. It all seemed endless, and we were clearly losing hope of winning, especially when we heard thunder rumble in the distance behind us. Had they tricked us by trapping us in the middle? When I turned my head to look at our doom, it wasn't the dark sorcerer's army trapping us in place, but the shiny gold armor of the Summer Court coming to our rescue.

When Drake approached, his eyes were fixed on me when he yelled, "We have to get you out of here!"

I threw my hands up in the air. "Don't you think I know that, you idiot!" I screamed back.

Oren came to my side. "We can't make it all the way back to the Winter Court with them coming after us. We need a plan."

"You're right," Drake replied, looking straight at me. I was furious at him, but the concern in his eyes gave me pause so I decided that for the time being I needed to be cooperative.

Quickly, I asked, "What should we do?"

Instead of responding to me, he turned to Oren and spoke to him. "We need a diversion. The dark sorcerer knows that you're her guardian. Wherever she is, you'll be there."

"And your point?" Oren asked impatiently.

"Sorcha comes with me and Sarette with you. She looks exactly like the princess so it should work. Head back fast to the Spring Court, it's much closer. Sorcha will come with me to Summer."

"What! No!" I demanded, cutting him off. "I'm not leaving my people!"

Oren looked torn, but reluctantly nodded at Drake. He turned to me and sighed. "It's the only way, *ai dulin*. You have a better chance of getting out of here, and he'll keep you safe."

Sarette grabbed my hand and squeezed. "Go! We'll be fine!"

"Switch weapons," Drake commanded, interrupting us. "They'll know your spear. If your friend has it they'll definitely think she's you."

I turned to him and growled. I hated being told what to do when I was going to do it in the first place. Sarette and I quickly switched weapons and began to move apart. Her sword felt odd in my hands, but I stashed it in my belt and bolted in the opposite direction from my friend and guardian.

"We need to hurry!" Drake exclaimed. "My people can't hold them off for much longer."

As the distance grew, I sent a silent prayer to Oren. *"Protect Sarette, and stay safe. Be careful, Oren."*

"Same to you, Princess. Get to the Summer Court safely."

My horse flew like the speed of light across the land, keeping up easily with Drake and his brown mare. The rumble of hooves on the ground signaled the advancement of the other Summer Fae warriors catching up to us. They surrounded me and Drake while we trekked the last few miles to the Summer Court. The air was hot and humid the moment we crossed into their territory, and it almost made me struggle to breathe it was so thick.

"Oren, I made it to Summer. Where are you?" I waited to hear him come through the connection, but I was only met with silence.

Drake stopped in front of the palace and climbed off his horse, looking relieved and worn out. I never knew he could look like that. Even in our dreams he was always calm and collected, never showing raw emotions. Climbing off my horse, I decided to try Oren again, desperate to hear his voice.

"Oren? Oren, where are you?"

Panic started to engulf me, and I struggled to breathe, gasping for air. Drake rushed over to me. "Are you hurt? What's wrong?" he asked,

72

surprisingly gentle.

He looked unsure of what to do and genuinely concerned, and in that moment I wanted to fall into his arms, but I couldn't. Instead, I fell to the ground screaming. The pain exploded in my mind, and I knew that it was Oren's pain coming through to me. He was hurt, and he was in distress. Tears streamed down my face as the pain intensified, bringing a whole new agony to the forefront. I felt like I was going to die.

"Something's wrong," I choked out, shocked that my body was losing control. Never before had I felt a tear, never before have I cried for someone, but in that moment … I cried.

Chapter Eight

DRAKE

Never in my life had I ever felt so helpless. Watching Sorcha scream in agony was the worst pain I thought I'd ever had to endure. My heart literally was ripped to shreds in that moment, and what was worse was that I had no clue how to help her. One of our healers had to use a sleeping spell on her to get her to calm down, and even then, her will was so strong that I thought the spell wouldn't work. She fought it for as long as she could, but eventually it became too much. I ended up watching her sleep for the rest of the afternoon. I never even took my eyes off of her when I heard someone enter the room through the door behind me.

"You need to get some rest, my Prince," the voice recommended. The healer who had cast the sleeping spell on Sorcha stood behind me. His name was Grayce, and he was one of the oldest faeries in our court.

"I'm not tired," I replied back, even though I felt

and looked exhausted.

"She's going to be asleep for a while, probably until tomorrow afternoon."

Wide-eyed, I peered back at the healer. "That long?" I asked hesitantly.

The healer looked thoughtful. "Unfortunately, yes, but she needed it."

Groaning, I put my head in my hands. "She may have needed it, but when she wakes up, all hell is going to break loose."

"What does that mean?" Grayce asked, looking confused.

Standing up, I ran my hands through my hair. "It means, master healer, that we're going to have a very angry Winter Fae woman on our hands."

My night was filled with a dreamless sleep. I assumed my subconscious listened to me when I said I didn't want to dream about Sorcha ever again. For the whole morning, I spent it with her at her bedside. Her warrior gear had been stripped, and she was cleaned and dressed in a beautiful blue robe. She always looked amazing in blue in my dreams, and even in real life she looked astonishing.

Sorcha looked like an angel lying there all peaceful and asleep, but I knew she was anything but one. The sleeping spell was probably about to wear off, so I decided that not being there would probably be best. I didn't want to be the source of her wrath. I was half tempted to lock the door to keep her from taking out her anger on an innocent passerby. I decided against it, but made sure to inform everyone to stay away from that part of the palace until she woke up.

I met my father in the throne room, along with the warriors that fought with me the day before. The grim expression on my father's face was answer enough. I was about to hear bad news.

"What news from the Spring Court? Did everyone make it there?" I asked, knowing very well that they didn't.

My father, King Oberon, shook his head and sighed. "Over half made it there, including Sorcha's brother, Brayden. He was badly injured, but Ariella is taking care of him while Meliantha makes her rounds to the wounded."

Closing my eyes, I asked the one question that I dreaded to hear the answer to. I had a feeling from Sorcha's episode earlier, her guardian and friend were in some serious trouble. "What about Sorcha's guardian and her friend?"

My father shook his head, and lowered his gaze.

"They didn't make it, son. We don't know if they're alive or dead."

Hanging my head, I groaned and ran my hands through my hair, frustrated. "How am I going to explain this to Sorcha? The minute she finds out she's going to want to leave here to find them, and I can't let her do that."

"You're absolutely right!" her voice hollered out. "I'm going to find them!" Lifting my head, I stood there frozen and shocked as Sorcha stood menacingly in the doorway to the throne room. She stalked toward me and my father, determination and confidence in each step.

"How are you feeling?" my father acknowledged her.

Sorcha grinned faintly and bowed her head. "Not too bad, actually. Thank you for your hospitality."

"You are most welcome, child. I'm sure you heard what we were discussing?"

Sorcha nodded. "Yes, and I wanted to tell you that I have a way to locate my guardian and Sarette. Once I find them, I'm going to go get them."

"I understand, and you know we'll help you," my father offered.

Curious, I asked, "What if your guardian is incapacitated and can't hear you through the bond? How will you know where they are, because obviously if he could tell you, you'd know by now?"

Narrowing her eyes, she gave me a sly grin. "I

have my ways, Prince Drake. By morning, I *will* know where they're at, and I *will* go to them. I refuse to let them suffer because of me." She bowed quickly to my father and me before hurrying out of the throne room. I wanted to follow her, but I couldn't bring myself to do it.

"She reminds me so much of her mother," my father uttered. He rose up from his throne and clapped me on the shoulder before leaving the room. Once all was quiet, I sat there in the throne room contemplating our next strategy plan. If Sorcha did, in some way, find out where her guardian was, there was only one way to get them out quickly and safely, and that way depended solely upon me.

After eating dinner with the warriors, we all dispersed to head to our beds for the evening. The warriors had their own quarters separate from the palace, but inside the walls just like me. I had my own dwelling that gave me the space and privacy away from my family, especially when Calista and Meliantha were still living there. I was almost outside the palace when the sound of music stopped me mid-step.

The music was achingly familiar, and the force of its pull had me turning around and ambling toward it. It was a sound that got my heart beating out of control and in pain from the sweet melody. I thought I'd never hear it again. It was the sound of Sorcha's song ... my song.

Chapter Nine

Sorcha

    The air in the Summer Court was different from the Winter; it was more vibrant and full of life. I loved my home, but something about being in the heart of Summer appealed to me. King Oberon had sent a message informing me of dinner, and invited me to join him and the queen. I politely declined, with deepest regrets, and ate alone in my room.

    I was wound up too tight and too apprehensive to sleep. My dreams were the only way I could communicate with Sarette and Oren, and if I couldn't calm myself down enough my attempts would be fruitless. Oren's mind was blocked or he was unconscious; either way, I was unable to talk to him every time I tried.

    Frustrated, I decided to walk around the palace to clear my mind. The curiosity in me piqued as I walked through the different halls of the palace, comparing it to my frigid home in the Winter. My eyes were alight with joy when I stumbled upon what had to have been their music room. The door was partially open, so it wasn't like I was *really* invading their privacy. Secretly, I pushed the door fully open and entered into heaven.

As I walked by the piano, I glided my fingers along the keys, careful not to make a sound. The instrument I was trying to get to lay in the corner of the room, looking desolate and alone. I bet no one ever played it. The harp was elegant and made of gold, whereas mine at home was made of silver. I took a deep breath before sitting on the stool and getting into position, praying they wouldn't be upset if I played it.

The chords were stiff as I played each note of my song ... the song I wrote for Drake. Closing my eyes, I let the music wash over me and take me to the place I kept hidden inside my soul, the place that only Drake was allowed to go. Once the song was completed, I sat there, letting the calmness of the melody soak through to my soul. I knew I was relaxed enough to do what I had to do.

Quietly, I left the music room and turned to head down the hall toward my bed chamber. Once I rounded the corner, I almost collided with the one person I wasn't expecting to see. Breathing hard, I stopped abruptly and placed a hand over my heart. "Drake, you scared me!" I shrieked.

"I'm sorry," he apologized, looking frantic. "Were you in the music room?"

Without thought or reason, I opened my mouth and lied, "No, I was just exploring your home. It's really nice by the way." With everything going on, I felt it was best to wait until things settled down before I told him the truth of our secret affair.

"The music," he whispered, looking away, confused. "I know I heard music." He lowered his head and ran his hands over his face. When his gorgeous gray gaze landed on mine, I melted where I stood, and almost buckled.

"I'm sorry, Drake," I said softly. "Maybe you just imagined the music you heard. The mind is a powerful place where our dreams can feel like reality, and you know what?" I said, looking deep into his eyes. "Most of the time those dreams come true. We just have to want them bad enough."

"Sorcha, what's going on? I've been trying to ignore the tension we have between us, but it's becoming unbearable. Your babbling doesn't help matters either. I don't know what's going on, or what the hell you're talking about, but I can see it in your eyes that you're keeping something from me."

He paused to study me, and it took all I had to bite my tongue about the babbling remark. He always gave me a hard time in our dreams when I was cryptic with my comments. It was one of the things I liked to do to drive him crazy. He reached up to touch my face like he was in a trance, but then blinked and pulled back quickly, clearing his throat. Softly, he said, "It's almost as if I've seen that look a million times on your face, but I don't see how that's possible. I don't even know you, but I'm having these weird feelings."

Taking a deep breath, I closed my eyes and hung my head, hiding my smile. When I opened them and lifted my head, the Drake from my dreams was there. I almost wrapped my arms around him, but stopped myself just in time. Drake caught the movement and frowned. It was getting harder to keep my distance with the pull tugging me to him.

Sighing, I explained, "I promise all will be revealed tomorrow. You may not understand what that means, but I need you to trust me. You'll find out everything soon enough, but for now I need to concentrate on finding Oren and Sarette without any distractions."

"Are you always this cryptic when you talk?"

Shrugging, I laughed. That was one of the first things he asked me in our dreams many moons ago. "Pretty much. I like to keep people on their toes, and keep them guessing."

A slow growing smile formed dangerously on his lips, and I ached to taste them like I'd done a thousand times in our dreams. When his eyes landed on my mouth, I licked my lips and wondered how much better things were going to taste and feel being outside of the dream realm. Silently, I groaned. He was such a bad influence on my body.

"These distractions you speak of ... do you consider me to be one or something?"

"Oh, yes." I sighed, feeling the flush creeping over my cheeks.

He laughed a deep, masculine laugh that sent chills down my body. "Do what you have to do, but I expect an explanation tomorrow, a real one."

Nodding, I whispered to him, "I promise to tell you everything tomorrow. My word is my bond." Without waiting for a reply, I walked past him and went straight to my room, breathing hard the entire way, wishing I could turn around and spend the rest of the night with him. Unfortunately, I couldn't. I had to concentrate on finding my guardian and Sarette.

Lying in my bed, thoughts of Drake seized my mind, but it didn't take long for sleep to take me away. I'd tried to get into Oren's head, but couldn't get a path to him. It was as if he was purposely blocked from my mind. Instead of probing further, I tried Sarette and amazingly got right in.

"Sorcha!" Sarette screamed, running to me. Not many people knew of my dream walking abilities, but

she did, which is why she didn't look shocked to see me. "I knew you would come," she cried, flinging her arms around me. "Please tell me Alston is with you."

I froze in her grasp, and so did she. From that one gesture she knew what my answer was going to be. "No," she whispered. "I saw him go down, but I knew he would get up, he had to have gotten up and gotten away. He just had to."

She was in denial, and my heart broke for her. After a few seconds, she sagged in my arms and started to cry. "I'm so sorry, Sarette, but he's not with me. I don't know where he is or if he even made it out alive." Grief consumed her, flowing in waves from her to me. Even though Alston and I had issues that brought me to hate him sometimes, I was still going to miss him. He was once my lover and friend, and would always hold a special place inside me no matter how our relationship ended.

"Sarette, I'm sorry I have to do this, but I need you to tell me where you are and what's going on. There will be plenty of time to grieve for Alston, but right now I need answers. Is Oren okay? He's not answering me when I speak to him."

"He'll be fine. He's out of it right now, but he'll live. His breathing is steady at least."

"Where are you?"

She shrugged. "I know we're near the Crystal Lake in the Mystical Forest. For the most part, I've been pretending to be incoherent, and keeping my head down. They think I'm you, but once they see my eyes and really get a good look at me they're going to know I'm not. I'm afraid of what they'll do when they find out."

"Is the dark sorcerer there?" I asked hesitantly.

She shook her head. "No, apparently he's not even in the Land of the Fae right now. The man who caught us is a dwarf named Brokk. He's the one Durin's been looking for, the same dwarf who delivered Meliantha's arrows and the cursed cuff that was given to Finn. Anyway, I heard him talking about how he wants to trade me for power. He says that if the dark sorcerer doesn't agree to the trade he's going to tell the courts where to find the sacred scroll."

My eyes went wide at that and she nodded weakly in return. I could tell that losing Alston was going to take a huge toll on her, but she was strong. I had to believe she'd get through it. Taking her by the shoulders, I made sure she was looking into my eyes when I spoke to her. "Okay, here's what we're going to do. When I wake up, I'm going to tell King Oberon and Drake everything so we can plan our attack. Whatever you do, keep your eyes hidden for as long as you can, but also try to keep tabs on the dwarf. I need to make sure we get him."

She nodded in understanding. "Just hurry, Sorcha. If the dark sorcerer comes back, things are going to get uglier and more complicated."

"Don't worry, I'm coming for you. As soon as I can get through to Oren I'll tell him what's going on. I just need you to be strong for me, and know that no matter what I will get you out of this," I assured her. We hugged one more time, and reluctantly, I let her go. Sarette smiled at me before the dream closed off and faded into black.

Once the dream was over, I flew out of the bed and into the night. I had to find Drake. I slept with my gear on, because I knew I wouldn't want to waste time once I had the information I needed. The heat flushed my skin the moment I stepped out of the palace doors, and immediately I began to sweat. The Summer Court was going to take time to get used to. I knew Drake didn't live inside the palace, but just outside of it in his own dwelling. It didn't take long to figure out which one was his, considering there was a dragon emblem on the front door.

Sunrise had to be only a couple of hours away, but I couldn't wait. We needed to get things going as soon as possible. I knocked on the door, and waited for him to answer. When he didn't come, I knocked harder and more persistent. The door snapped open, revealing a half-naked Drake with a scowl on his face, and hair mussed up from sleep. I gawked at him like a starved animal, and couldn't stop my eyes from taking him all in. His tanned muscles were sculpted to his lean body, and when he caught me staring, an amused smirk came across his face and he flexed his muscles. That brought me out of my stupor.

"Let's go! I know where they're at," I blurted out. "We need to get to them quickly."

"Calm down," he murmured gently. "We'll get them out safely. Go to the throne room and I'll have everyone there in ten minutes."

Turning on my heel, I raced back up to the palace and into the throne room. I had ten minutes to get my bearings before all my secrets were revealed to the whole Summer Court, and to Drake. The room was alight with candles and smelled fragrantly of sunshine and flowers, but no amount of sweet smells were going to calm my nerves. I paced for the full ten minutes it took to get everyone assembled. They were all eager and ready for battle.

King Oberon took his place at the front and sat while Drake stood up beside him, both waiting for me to speak. Quickly, I glanced around the room at everyone present before I began. Loudly, I spoke so the whole room could hear me. "I was able to get into contact with my friend and guardian last night. I know where they're at, and what's going on. It's not what I was expecting."

King Oberon nodded. "Go on, Princess. We're all listening."

Sneaking a glance at Drake, he nodded as well.. "Apparently, there's been a mutiny of sorts with some of the dark sorcerer's people. The man in charge of the attack is a dwarf named Brokk, and he's the one Durin's been searching for since the whole Meliantha debacle. He thinks Sarette is me, and he wants to trade my power *for* power. If the dark sorcerer doesn't grant him this, Brokk is going to threaten to tell the courts where he hid the secret scroll, the same scroll our people wrote over a century ago telling us how to defeat him. It seems the dark sorcerer wasn't the only one who knew where the scroll was hidden."

Gasps erupted from everyone, and the feeling of hope we never thought imaginable surged with great force throughout the room. We've been searching for years to find a way to defeat Alasdair, and his evil magic, and we were so close to finding it.

King Oberon raised his hand. Everything and everyone went silent. "If this is true, then we need to find out where the scroll is at."

I agreed. "If we capture Brokk and bring him here I can find out everything we need to know."

The king furrowed his brow in question. "How?" he asked.

Here we go, I thought.

"As you know, when one of the Four come into

89

their full power some new abilities emerge. Calista is the all-powerful, Meliantha can heal and bring back life, and I can find the truth. I'm a truthseeker."

Drake took that time to speak. "How does that work?" he asked curiously.

"All I need is to have contact to him, like touching his hand and so forth, and the answers will come to me."

"And this was your guardian that told you all of this?" King Oberon asked.

I paused and inhaled deeply, knowing it was the time I was going to reveal my secret. Slowly letting out my deep breath, I finally answered, "No … it wasn't my guardian, but my friend, Sarette, who told me."

The king paused, weighing in my reply. "How is that possible? It doesn't make any sense," he remarked.

The time had come, and instead of answering the King, I looked straight at Drake when I spoke. "It's possible because I visited her in her dreams. You see … not only am I a truth seeker, but I'm a dream walker as well."

Drake's mouth flew open and uncertainty crossed his features. I could tell by the expression on his face that he was wondering if our dreams were real or if he cooked them up in his own imagination. If he asked in front of his people and I said that it wasn't me he would feel like a fool in front of them.

King Oberon looked pleased. "I'm impressed, Princess. The only other person I know with dream walking abilities is Elvena, but she needs others to help her. Are you saying you can do it all by yourself?"

"Yes, Your Highness."

"You and my daughters have become very powerful women. No wonder the dark sorcerer wants you. Let's pray we have better luck keeping you out of his grasp. Sometimes it seems the more we tried keeping my daughters safe, the easier it was for the dark sorcerer to get to them." The king's eyes looked haunted and weary. I knew he had to feel like he failed when the dark sorcerer took Calista and Meliantha's power.

"Let's hope so," I agreed. "What do we do now?" I asked, turning to Drake.

He returned my gaze and stared at nothing except me for a few seconds, but then looked across the room at the warriors. "We need to leave now while it's still dark. That way I'll be concealed when I fly overhead to scout out the army. I want you to divide into two groups and come at them from different areas while I come in from the sky. Do you all understand?" he commanded, his voice booming across the room.

"Aye!" the warriors agreed in unison.

"Then let's go!"

At Drake's dismissal everyone dispersed,

including me. Swiftly, I turned around and raced out of the throne room and the palace doors.

"Sorcha!" Drake yelled.

My steps faltered for a moment, but I kept walking. There were too many people around, and I didn't want to discuss anything with him while the warriors were there to witness it. Not to mention what would happen if he touched me.

"Sorcha, stop!"

Before I could make it to the secluded garden on the other side of the palace, I was taken by the arm by Drake's warm, solid grasp. That touch was all it took.

The Vision

The sound of waves crashing around me brings comfort to my ears as I swim along in the crystal blue depths of my sea ... the Summer Sea. The Land of the Fae has changed—grown—bringing a whole new Summer Court. I have never understood the magic of the land, except all I know is that it gifted us with a whole new life ... a whole new land. We're separate from the original Summer Court, but we're still one and the same. However, this part belongs to me and Drake.

The water feels cool against my heated skin, except when I see the smoky gray eyes of the man before me, the water quickly heats up. I could feel the current of it around me pulling him closer, as if it knew that's where he belonged ... in my arms. When Drake grasps me against his naked body, he takes my face in his hands and wastes no time in claiming me as his own. The sea churns and moves frantically around us as Drake kisses me hungrily, feverishly. His lips taste salty from the water, but underneath that is the pure and exotic taste of the Summer. It's addicting. He is addicting.

The sea appears to know our needs and wants, and is obviously reflecting our moods. Right now the water is wild and dangerous, flowing excitedly around us, caressing our bodies. Our passions are fierce and full of heat, just like the sea. I can see the fire burning in Drake's eyes, and it makes my blood boil. Wrapping my legs around his waist, he gently strokes my opening with the head of his cock before plunging in deeply with one hard thrust. I scream out in pleasure as he rocks my body against the waves. Before, I never welcomed the heat, but now I live in it … and I love it. This is my home, and this is where I belong.

Chapter Ten

DRAKE

The moment I was thrust out of the vision everything became clear. Sorcha swayed on her feet, but I caught her, earning me a dazed smile in return. "Of all the days for this to happen, it had to be on one where we're going into battle," she said sarcastically.

I laughed. "You should know things are never easy here, especially when you're one of the Four. Take my sisters for example."

"Yeah, I guess you're right," she agreed.

Sorcha lowered her head and stared at the ground nervously, a trait I'd never seen from her before. There were so many questions floating through my mind and I didn't know where to start. "So, are you going to tell me everything now?" I asked, trying hard to hide my desperation.

With a smirk on her face, she lifted her head and beamed. "I think you know everything, Drake."

After hearing about her dream walking abilities I pretty much knew then that my dreams were real, but I wanted to hear it all from her. "Yes, but I want to hear you say it to me."

Taking a deep breath, she let it out slowly and pierced me with her emerald green gaze. "Very well then. Where do you want me to start?"

"I want you to start with the dreams. Were they *all* real? Was it really you in them *every* single night? And most importantly, what the hell were you doing with me when you were obviously with that dickhead?" I asked, crossing my arms over my chest. I wasn't angry before, but now that I knew the truth I was pissed knowing she came to me in my dreams and also shared a bed with Alston at the same time.

She lowered her head and laughed. "There's no need to get angry. There hasn't been a 'me and Alston' for a long time now." When she looked up at me I could see the honesty in her eyes. I should've known he would lie to me, and I was stupid to believe him.

"That's not what he said," I said flatly.

She huffed out a breath. "Son of a bitch! Is that why you looked pissed yesterday?" she asked. At my nod, she continued, "I should have known he would do something like that. I guess he didn't get over your pissing contest at the Winter Ball."

"Hey, he started it," I pointed out with a smile on my face.

Shaking her head, a sadness grew over her face and her lips turned down in a frown. "It doesn't matter now. I think he's dead, Drake. Sarette said she saw him go down in the fight, but she was hoping he was with us. I told her that he wasn't."

"I'm sorry, Sorcha. I didn't like the guy, but I know he was your friend," I said, hugging her tight. Even though Alston was a dick, I would never have wished death on him.

"Anyway, answering your *other* questions, yes the dreams were all real. From the first time I visited you in your dreams, I couldn't stop. I kept telling myself not to go back, but I didn't listen." She lifted her gaze and smiled mischievously. "I guess I liked fighting with you too much."

I laughed. "That's it? We did a lot more in our dreams than fight."

In my dreams, I touched and kissed her every night. It was all real ... our love was real. Sorcha smiled when she caught me staring at her lips, and ran her tongue over them enticingly. We had a strong connection in our dreams, but being this close to her in person has intensified that bond. Lifting my hand, I ran it through her silky black tresses before grazing her pale cheek with my finger. Her skin was as white as snow, but soon it would be the color of Summer.

"Are you wanting to kiss me, Drake?" she asked humorously.

"Maybe," I answered, moving closer. "Are you against me kissing you, because if I recall correctly, I think we've done a little more than that in our dreams."

She smiled and bit her lip. "Oh yes," she sighed. "How could I forget?"

Groaning, I instantly grew hard at the thought of the vision and our time together. If we didn't have to rescue her people, I'd lay her down right where we were and make love to her all damn night. Placing my hands on her face, I pulled her toward me to close that last inch. She moaned and smiled wickedly at me when she felt my hard cock pressed and ready for action against her leg. To make matters worse, she tortured me by gliding her leg up and down it, making me groan and grip her hips rousingly.

When our lips touched, it was like nothing I'd ever felt before. I'd kissed her in our dreams, but nothing could compare to what her body felt like against mine. I could feel the beginnings of our bond take place as we kissed, and I knew in that moment that things were about to change. It happened to my sisters and I knew it was happening right that second.

Sorcha must had felt it too because she abruptly pulled away from the kiss and gasped. Lifting up her hands, she turned them back and forth in awe. "It's happening," she whispered.

I was amazed at how one minute she was the cold, pale Winter princess, and then the next her skin started changing before my eyes, turning into the sun-kissed golden of Summer. My skin, however, stayed the same. Confused, Sorcha picked up my hands and examined my unchanged flesh.

"Why isn't anything happening to you?"

I was pretty sure I knew the answer to that. "It's because I'm Summer, Sorcha. I will always be a Summer Fae. It's where I belonged the moment I was born, but I can feel the change starting *inside* me and it feels amazing."

"Drake!" someone yelled from behind me.

When I turned, I found my second in command, Finn, running toward us. Finn had been Meliantha's lover for a few years while the dark sorcerer made fools of us all. Even though Finn still loved my sister back then, he chose to stay in the Summer Court and be my second in command instead of following her.

"The warriors are ready. We're waiting for your command," he claimed.

Nodding, I acknowledged him. "Excellent! Go ahead and ride toward Crystal Lake. Once I get changed, I'll fly overhead."

Finn bowed and sprinted back to the front of the palace while Sorcha and I followed soon after him. "Which group will I be riding with?" she asked as we made our way to the front.

"Neither," I replied.

Immediately, her eyes grew fierce and she stopped, placing her hands on her hips. "You're not going to stop me from going. Don't you dare turn into an overprotective jackass to go along with your arrogant side. I can only handle one of those traits."

Laughing, I took her hand and pulled her along

with me. "Trust me, I know better than to tell you what to do. I think I learned my mistake once already in one of our dreams."

"Just as long as you remember it," she teased. Stopping mid-step, she grabbed my arm, halting me. "So, if I'm not riding with the warriors, where will I be?"

"With me." I grinned. "Up in the air, and on my back." Her eyes went wide and her mouth flew open in surprise. Nudging her with my elbow, I winked. "Don't look so shocked. You knew you were going to ride me at some point."

She lifted her brow at the remark, making me laugh, but then she turned serious. "I'm sure you would like for me to ride you, but that's not what we're talking about. Seriously, I didn't realize it would be so soon. It's not every day a girl gets to ride on the back of a dragon. What if I fall off?"

Taking her face in my hands, I kissed her long and deep, relishing in the way she already tasted like a Summer Fae. "You will never fall as long as you're with me. I will spend every day, every hour, and every waking minute of my life keeping you safe. Just trust me."

"I do," she confessed wholeheartedly.

"Okay, first things first, when I change into the dragon don't be afraid. I would never hurt you. When the change is complete just climb on my back and hold on."

"Sounds good," she agreed, bouncing on her heels.

I backed away from her slowly and began taking off my clothes. She kept watch the whole time, running her green gaze over my body with a smile on her face. "Enjoy it being one-sided right now, because when we get back you're going to be in this same position. Our dreams will soon be coming true," I added, winking.

She shook her head and waved her hands impatiently. "I look forward to it, but you need to hurry up! We've wasted too much time. My friends need us. I feel guilty enough as it is ogling you while they're in danger."

Once the change started, Sorcha's eyes grew wide in concern, and she cringed. Watching the transformation was hard the first time, or at least that's what I'd noticed. It took Ariella a few times to get used to it. After the transformation was complete, I stood at my full height while Sorcha gazed up at me, mesmerized. I lowered myself to her, waiting for her to climb on my back. She hesitated for a few seconds, but then climbed up and settled her body at the base of my neck.

"You are so beautiful," she murmured in awe, running her hands over my scaly dragon skin. I huffed in response, and looked back at her. When she was fully secured and hanging on tight, she gave me the final nod. "I'm ready," she assured me.

The moment I took off into the sky I could feel her tense up and hold tighter. No matter what happened, we were going to rescue her friend and guardian, and I was going to keep her safe. She was *mine* ... mine to protect.

The Crystal Lake was quickly coming upon us, and thankfully, the early morning darkness concealed me in the sky, giving me full advantage. My enhanced vision helped me see through the trees to the army below. Everyone was mostly still, but there were a few people up and about, completely unaware of what was approaching. I knew one thing ... they were going to run like spineless cowards by the time I got through with them.

Circling quietly around the camp, I waited for my army to get closer, and when they came into sight I descended down on the enemy, letting out a guttural roar with fire from the depths inside me.

Chapter Eleven

Sorcha

Drake's growl was ear-piercingly loud, and if I didn't know it was him I would've cowered in fear. I wasn't afraid of him in his dragon form, but just the knowledge of what he could do was a bit terrifying. It had to be wonderful yet lonely to be the only dragon in the Land of the Fae.

"Oren? Can you hear me?"

Silence was all I heard as a reply, and it scared me. I would know if he was dead, but the silence wasn't normal. Even though the wind whipping by us was loud, I knew Drake could hear me when I called out to him, "Sarette told me they were in the middle of the camp tied to a post. The dwarf we need to capture is the one with my spear. We just need to find him and take him down."

Drake landed with a hard thud onto the land below, almost making me lose my grip. The sound roused the dark sorcerer's army, and almost instantly they were alert and ready to fight. Pulling out

Sarette's sword, I headed into the fray, ready for battle. The screams and grunts of the fighting were all I heard as I killed one faerie after the other. The sword felt odd in my hands, but I was well trained in how to use it. I was in a zone where nothing and no one mattered except my friend and guardian. Death was a consequence the traitors knew would happen if they turned against their people.

Anger and betrayal overwhelmed me as more and more of my fellow fae came for the attack, and as much as I hated to kill them I knew I had to. As more faeries and fae creatures fell, I could see through the crowd to the center of the camp. Sarette was struggling against her bonds while Oren stayed limp at her side. Drake slashed his way through the enemy, severing limbs and bodies in the process while making me a clear path to my friends.

"Sarette!" I screamed, running toward her. "Are you okay?"

In the next instant, I heard before I felt the arrow slicing through the air and landing its target. The next step I took had me reeling in agony. White, hot fire surged through my veins as pain engulfed every cell of my being. I collapsed to my knees as Drake bellowed out a roar behind me. Jutting out from my shoulder blade was a deeply embedded arrow, and it hurt.

"What the hell!" I yelled, angry and pissed for getting hit. Staggering along the way, I eventually reached Sarette and Oren, and using my good arm I cut their bonds, releasing them.

Sarette was frantic. "Holy shit! Sorcha, are you okay? Turn around!" she demanded. As soon as I turned around she ripped the arrow out of my shoulder with one sharp pull. Screaming loudly, I fell to my knees on the ground and clutched my bad shoulder. Drake nudged me in the side, concerned.

"I'm okay, Drake. It just hurt that's all."

Fire shot through his nostrils as he scanned the woods for the attacker, emanating danger and death. Sarette spotted the culprit first and pointed to the trees. "It's him!" Sarette shouted. "Sorcha, it's Brokk, the one we need!"

Once Drake understood, he bounded through the trees, knocking them down in the process, as he chased after the dwarf. Needless to say, the dwarf didn't get far. In one massive swipe, Drake brought his claws back and hit Brokk so hard he went flying in the air. It just so happened that he landed knocked out at my feet with my spear attached to his back and a bow in hand.

I kicked the bow out of his grasp, grabbed my spear, and dropped to my knees beside Oren. Running my hands over his body, I couldn't see or feel any massive injuries. *What could be keeping him under?* I wondered.

Finn, who happened to be nearby, rushed over to help. "Princess, are you all right? You're bleeding."

Breathless, I nodded weakly. "I'll be fine. I don't know what's wrong with my guardian, but he needs help." Glaring at the unconscious dwarf, I continued while pointing at him, "That piece of shit there needs to be questioned, and taken back to the Summer Court. We need to contact Durin and have him there as well. This is the dwarf he's been looking for."

"Will do, Your Highness," Finn agreed. "We'll secure him and head straight for the Summer Court. The enemy is mostly dead, except for the few that retreated during the attack."

Despair washed through me at the thought of so many killed. I wondered how many of those fae were actual traitors, and ones that were forced to be there. Either way, the damage was done, and I had to live with not knowing. Finn picked Brokk up and strapped him to a horse, making the bonds tighter than usual across the dwarf's limbs. *Good,* I thought. *He deserved it.* He was going to have a lot more pain after I was done with him.

Sarette helped me haul Oren across Drake's back, and once he was settled I climbed behind him so I could hold him in place. Sarette clambered up behind me and held on tight. "We're ready, Drake! Let's go!" I called out to him.

In one quick jump we were up and in the sky. My shoulder ached, and I winced when I tried to move my arm. Now that the adrenaline had ebbed off I was feeling more of the burn. Blood oozed warm and hot down my back, and I could feel my body swaying.

"Sorcha! Sorcha, what's wrong?" Sarette screamed worriedly in my ear, and even though she was right behind me, she sounded amazingly far away. My vision grew blurry, and then it slowly began to grow dark. There was no pain … just peace.

Bright light streamed through the open window, making me squint and hide my face with the pillow. Groaning, I turned over on my side, but quickly sat up as the realization dawned on me. The pain in my shoulder was still there, but it wasn't bad. Earlier, I was in the air with Drake, but now I was in a bed … with Drake. *What the hell happened?* I wondered. I glanced over to see him sleeping peacefully in the bed beside me. His tousled red hair and half-naked body beckoned me to touch him, and for the first time he actually looked normal. Not the infamous and arrogant prince dragon, but just a normal man.

He must've known I was staring at him because a slow growing smile appeared on his face. He sat up and ran his eyes over my body, clearly admiring the little silky get up I was wearing. I was out of my warrior gear, and placed in a blue lingerie-type night gown, most likely compliments of the man beside me. My golden skin stood out against the light blue color of the silk, and it still amazed me how much I had changed within just a day. Not just physically, but emotionally as well.

"Good morning, beautiful. Or better yet, good afternoon. I thought you were going to sleep all day."

Confused, I asked, "What happened? How long was I out?"

Drake sat up and tucked a loose strand of hair behind my ear. "You passed out when we were in the air. With all the excitement and blood loss you must've just given out. You've only been asleep for a few hours. I didn't want to leave you, so I stayed here."

"What about Oren?" I asked, panicking. "Where is he? Is he all right?"

As soon as I said his name, Oren came barreling into the room. "Did I hear someone call out my name?" he asked, charging toward me with a huge smile on his face. He scooped me up in his arms, but let me go when I winced in pain. "I'm sorry, *ai dulin*. I didn't mean to hurt your shoulder. It's just so good to see you again." He hugged me gently and kissed my forehead. "You have no idea how helpless I felt the whole time. I knew you were safe, but there was nothing I could do if anything happened to Sarette. I would've failed you."

Shaking my head, I took his face in my hands. "It doesn't matter now. We're all here and we're safe. I was so worried about you. What happened? Why were you unconscious the way you were?" I asked.

Oren took a seat on the bed and placed his head in his hands. I could tell he was uncomfortable with feeling the way he did about what happened. I was just glad he was safe and in one piece. He explained, "I don't know everything, but someone had cast a sleeping spell on me. Apparently, they didn't want me conversing 'in secret' with Sarette, who was supposed to be you. They didn't want us communicating and planning an escape."

"How did you get out of it?"

Oren smiled and motioned toward Drake. "His healer, Grayce, had gotten me out of it. He also helped with your wound. They had to shove some nasty tasting herbal mess down my throat that tasted like horse dung. Although, I guess it worked." He laughed while I made a disgusted face.

"That sounds pretty gross, indeed. Is Sarette okay?" I asked, looking back and forth from my guardian to Drake.

Oren answered, "Ever since we got back she's been grieving over Alston. She's having a hard time right now, and refuses to talk about it."

"I can imagine," I announced sadly. "I'll try to talk to her. What about Brokk? Has he talked yet?"

Oren shook his head. "Not yet. We're waiting on

Durin to get here. They're going to need you, too. If anyone can find out the information we need it's you."

Anger flashed through me as the pain from my wound sparked again. "You're damn right it's going to be me. If he doesn't cooperate he's going to have some really nasty nightmares, and I'm going to love giving them to him. Besides, I owe him some pain." I smiled deviously.

Drake laughed and kissed me softly on the lips. If Oren wasn't watching I would've deepened the kiss, and probably done more if my shoulder wasn't hurting. "Remind me never to get on your bad side," Drake confessed.

"Oh, you've been there, and even though you've pissed me off I still never had the desire to hurt you the way I could hurt others."

"And for that I'm thankful," Drake admitted sheepishly. "Do you think you're ready to work your magic?"

Confident, I nodded. "More than ready."

Brokk was seated in the throne room surrounded

by multiple warriors, including King Oberon and Drake, while Durin and I congregated outside to go through our game plan. Durin, the leader of the dwarves, just arrived and wanted an update so I filled him in on what I planned to do. Durin exuded power and was definitely a force to be reckoned with. He stood about four foot tall with closely cut brown hair, and was built with pure muscle. He was a confident man who never once balked when people had to look down at him. His confidence made him appear as if he was a giant, and he was also well respected. Most of the dwarves were hairy and smelled very musky at times, but Durin was different. He was closely shaven and neatly dressed every time I saw him, and never smelled bad. His warm hazel eyes could see through anyone's soul, or at least that's how it felt when he would look at you. They were intense. There were several women on our council who fawned over him every time he visited, and I was sure that was why he made it a point to come talk to my father, King Madoc.

"When I ask him questions, what do you have to do to find out if he's telling the truth?" Durin asked.

"If I touch him or if I'm close to him I can usually tell that way. It all depends on how strong his feelings are. If it gets really complicated I'll have to go about this in another way. What do you know about Brokk? What is he afraid of?" I asked curiously. I needed to know what to do if I had to invade his dreams.

Durin was lost in thought for a moment, but then he answered, "He hates the water. He almost drowned one time after he fell into one of the lakes. His armor kept dragging him down. Ever since then, before he left our lands, he stayed away from the water."

Smiling devilishly, I was ready for the mind games. "Let's do this, but first, I want to introduce myself to him ... the Winter Court way."

Durin chuckled. "Have fun, Princess. I had a feeling you'd want to make him pay for shooting you." I answered with a wink.

When the doors opened, Durin and I walked in together. Brokk's eyes went wide at the sight of his leader, but then he turned smug and unreadable. He wanted us to think he wasn't scared, but I saw the tremble in his body when we first walked in. The cool and calm look on Brokk's face only spurred my anger even more, making my steps furious and hard against the marble floors as I approached him. Once he was within striking distance, I reared my arm back and punched him so hard in the face I could feel bones crack. The pain in my shoulder sent a wave of agony through my body, but I didn't show any sign of weakness even though I was sweating like crazy from the igniting pain.

Brokk's chair fell back, tumbling him awkwardly to the floor. Trying to hide their smiles, a couple of the warriors bent down to right Brokk's chair with him strapped helplessly to it. Blood ran down his face, and I couldn't bite back the smile even if I wanted to.

"Hello Brokk. It's nice to meet you, especially now that I don't have an arrow sticking out of my back."

Brokk grimaced. "That was a mistake. I didn't know it was you. I thought you were the one strapped to the post."

"Oh, you better be glad that wasn't me," I warned darkly, sidling closer so he could see the promise in my eyes. "Because if it was me, little dwarf, I would've ripped you limb to limb and enjoyed every single glorious scream that came from your traitorous mouth. No one hurts my people and gets away with it."

With that, I slowly backed up and let Durin take over. Brokk's feelings were everywhere, and since I already had contact with his flesh I was confident I'd be able to read him clearly from a short distance away. Drake left his father's side and joined me by mine. Leaning over, he whispered in my ear, "Nice work, beautiful. You looked sexy as hell out there. I was about to have to fight off my warriors if you kept it up. You should've seen the way they were all salivating over you. Do I need to mark my territory?"

Wrapping my arms around his neck, I pulled him down to place a tender kiss against his lips. He instantly crushed me to him and kissed me back fiercely earning several gasps from the crowd. I laughed when he released my lips, realizing why he did what he did. If anyone else tried to do that they would be sprawled out on the floor in pain, but with Drake claiming me it felt right.

"I guess you just marked your territory," I said, smiling. "I actually find it kind of hot that you want to mark me as yours, but you have nothing to worry about. I will *always* be yours." He grinned and kissed me again before turning his attention back to Durin and Brokk.

"Are you ready, Princess?" Durin asked. Nodding, I walked over and stood a couple of feet behind Brokk so he wouldn't be able to see me.

"What is she doing?" Brokk demanded, turning his head, trying to see me.

"That is none of your concern," Durin responded smoothly. "I need to ask you some questions and you're going to answer them. First, where's the dark sorcerer?"

Brokk grumbled, "I don't know, the Black Forest perhaps."

It was a bold-faced lie, and I could've felt the treachery in it a mile away. I shook my head so Durin would know it was a false answer.

Durin lowered his head and clucked his tongue impatiently. "Lies will get you nowhere, Brokk. Without my protection, the dark sorcerer will surely come for your head."

Brokk shrugged. "I'm dead anyway. So again, I'll tell you nothing."

"Sorcha?" Durin called out, gritting his teeth. "Instead of wasting valuable time why don't we go with your plan? I'm sure it'll be way more effective."

I agreed. "I think you're right." I left my spot to stand before Brokk. His eyes were wide and unsure, the smell of fear emanated off of him in thick waves. "Are you sure you don't want to answer the questions we ask?" I asked the dwarf.

He snarled, "I would rather rot."

Anger coursed through me, and I reacted instantly, letting that rage guide me. Placing my hands on each arm rest and caging him in, I bent down until I was only a few inches from his face. My tone was low and cruel when I whispered, "What are you afraid of, Brokk? You see, I may appear as a weak female to you, but I can do things that would fuck up that little mind of yours in a heartbeat. Even if I have to do it every night of your life I will, and I'll enjoy it, too."

"What are you talking about?" Brokk snapped hesitantly.

"I'm talking about getting into your dreams, little dwarf. Plaguing your mind with fears and insecurities while you piddle along scared shitless. Take for instance, your abhorrence of water ..." His smugness left and was replaced with genuine dread. A wicked smile took over my face because I knew I triumphed.

"Do you want to drown every night in your dreams? Because I can surely make that happen. Or better yet, do you have a family? How would you like to see them suffer every night because of your greediness for power?"

"Stop!" he demanded. Sweat broke out on his forehead; his eyes were wild and his breathing was frantic. "You are one heartless bitch!" he shouted in anger.

I wasn't happy with what I said to him, and I'd never torture someone's family in their dreams. Being cruel like that was never something I did, even to people that deserved it, but I had to use a scare tactic with him.

Shrugging my shoulders, I looked at Brokk impassively. "I'm the daughter of the Ice Queen. What did you expect ... flowers and bunnies? This is the last time we're going to ask before I start the real fun. Will you answer my questions or not?" I asked.

His silence was answer enough, so I backed up and sighed. "Okay, I guess it's time to put your lights out. Goodnight, little dwarf, I'll see you soon."

The warriors stationed around Brokk slowly started moving in. Hands were raised and fists were about to fly. Before the first hit could make its way, Brokk yelled out in defeat. "Stop! I'll talk. I promise I'll talk, just tell them to back up!"

The warriors stepped aside while I smiled smugly at Brokk. "I'm glad you could see reason. All right, first question. Where is the dark sorcerer?"

Releasing a heavy breath, Brokk answered, "He's in the mortal realm." *Truth.*

"Why?" I countered.

"Because he wants to recruit mortals since they can wield iron." *Truth.*

Angry cries and shouts erupted throughout the room, and this time Drake spoke. "He can't bring mortals here. Their weapons could endanger us all."

Brokk nodded. "That's one of his plans." *Truth.*

"Why did you turn on your people?" I asked.

Durin moved closer to hear the answer, looking wary in the process. Brokk noticed, but turned his eyes downward when he revealed his confession. "My wife thought I was weak. When I almost drowned she thought it was a pathetic way to die. She wanted me to redeem myself and our family name of its embarrassment. I had no clue how to do that without power. I was a nobody in the ranks, just a simple messenger." *Truth.*

Both Durin and I deflated hearing Brokk's admission. It was raw and hurtful, and I could feel the pain coming off of him. As much as I pitied him, he still shouldn't have turned to the dark sorcerer. That was the wrong choice. "I'm sorry about that," I admitted, meaning every word. "No man should have to hear that from his wife, especially after you went through your ordeal, but it doesn't make what you did right. Once you leave here you'll be in Durin's possession, but if you answer my next questions truthfully you'll be redeemed by the Winter Court."

Defeated, Brokk sighed and hung his head. "What else do you need to know?"

"Where is the sacred scroll?" I asked.

Terrified, he glanced up quickly. "How do you know about that?" When I didn't answer, he groaned and explained, "The scroll is hidden at the highest peak in the Endelyn Mountains. No one can travel there by foot so the dark sorcerer thought it best to hide it there. It's hidden inside a wooden box, and buried under a pile of rocks. With your powers you'll be able to sense its location." *Truth*.

Narrowing my eyes, I searched his face. There was something he wasn't telling us. It couldn't be that easy to get the scroll. "What else, Brokk? What's the catch? It can't be that easy."

"It's not," he confessed. "The box it's in is surrounded by magic. It takes great power to open it, and so far the only ones powerful enough to do that are one of the Four … you. Your blood will open it."

"Well, then I guess I'll be the one searching for the box," I said.

"You can't fly. There's no way you can get there."

"That's why she'll have me," Drake piped in, coming to my side. "I'll get her there safely." He wrapped his arm around my shoulder and squeezed. "We can add it to our list of adventures."

"That's sweet, but you're missing the point," Brokk said dryly. "When the princess gives her blood to open the box that magic she gives will go straight to the dark sorcerer. You see, the magic surrounding the box is connected to the talisman. He *will* get her power if you do this, which means he'll be one step closer to being the most powerful being in this realm."

Silence filled the room as the information of what he just said soaked in. No one moved and not a sound came from any of them, but I could see the mixture of expressions on their faces. Some wanted the scroll while others didn't want the dark sorcerer getting any closer to being invincible. I had no choice, *we* had no choice. If I didn't give up my power we'd never know how to defeat the dark sorcerer.

"You can't do this, Sorcha," Drake demanded fiercely. "We'll figure out another way."

Sadly, I knew there wasn't. "There is no other way. I have to do this, and you're coming with me."

"Why are you so damn stubborn?"

Leaning forward, I kissed him on the lips and smiled. "It's because I was made to keep you on your toes, and vice versa."

He gave in and laughed. "You're damn right, and don't you forget it."

"How could I?" I quipped happily.

Now that the truth was spilled, Durin took Brokk

and they left the Summer Court to head back to Endelyn, their home. I didn't know what punishment Durin had planned for Brokk, and it wasn't my place to ask, so I didn't. The dwarves had their own form of punishment.

Now that the meeting was over, Drake escorted me to my room after asking Oren if he wouldn't mind if he did so, alone. At my nod, Oren left and went to his chamber. When we got to my room, Drake turned to face me and took both of my hands in his.

"Stay with me tonight," he whispered softly. The need in his voice, plus the magnetic pull drawing me closer to him, had me flush with his body and breathing in his glorious scent. He smelled of Summer, of a time spent dancing in the sun and also the exotic scent of the ferocity below his skin.

"Where? At your place or here in my room?" I asked. His steely gray eyes were serious and full of longing. Ever since I'd been in contact with him it's been one problem after another. We hadn't had any alone time just to be with each other. With everything going on, I hadn't realized how much I craved it.

"I want you to stay with me … in my home, away from the distractions here. I know we've gotten to know everything about each other in our dreams, but now I want to feel it. I want to feel you wrapped in my arms, and know it's real."

"Okay," I breathed. "But I don't know if I can trust myself with you."

He smiled that sinful smile of his and bent down to kiss me. I opened for him willingly, allowing his tongue to caress mine. Groaning, I pressed into him harder, making him tighten his hold around me. I could feel him harden against my leg, and I ached to feel him again, to seal the bond that we've been meant to fulfill since the beginning of time.

"Drake?" I whispered hoarsely once he released my lips. He trailed his tongue across my jaw over to my ear, where he bit lightly on the tender flesh, causing me to whimper.

"Hmm …"

"We need to get out of here before someone sees."

His masculine laugh sounded dangerous in my ear, sending chill bumps crawling over my skin. In his low, deep voice he murmured in my ear, "Come on. Let's get something to eat and head to my place. You can take a shower there as well, and if you're lucky maybe I'll join you."

When he pulled back he winked at me and grinned devilishly. Heat flushed through my body at the thought of us in the shower together, lathering and washing each other clean. My body craved him like it craved food and water. How was I going to handle a whole night alone with him?

"We'll see," I teased.

Grabbing my hand, he held it all the way to the kitchen where we grabbed a couple of plates of food the brownies had prepared. Once outside, the Summer humidity drenched my skin, but it didn't bother me anymore. My blood was changing, and soon the Summer Court would be my home. I wanted to find Sarette and talk to her, but I needed this time with Drake.

Once we reached his dwelling, he opened the door and ushered me inside. His place smelled amazingly like him, all Summer and pure male. I set my plate on his table and took the tour of his house, intentionally bypassing his bedroom for the time being.

When I was done exploring, Drake was waiting for me and pulled out a chair for me to sit in at the table. "Thank you," I said as I sat down. The food smelled amazing and I couldn't wait to devour it. "How old were you when you decided to have your own place? I don't remember you ever telling me in our dreams."

He rubbed his chin in concentration and leaned back casually in his chair. "If I'm not mistaken, I was seventeen when I came to stay out here. My sisters used to drive me crazy, especially Calista."

I smiled thinking about how my brothers probably got annoyed with me, too. "Out of all your sisters, who do you mostly relate to?"

"That's easy … Ariella. Now that she's older she's grown on me. I've never seen anyone fluster my warriors like she does, and for some crazy reason she always knows what I'm thinking. I'm starting to think she should've been my twin instead of Calista."

"You have a lovely family. I adore Meliantha. I felt bad for pushing Kalen to be with Breena after that horrible mess with the dark sorcerer. I didn't realize my friend was a traitorous whore," I added vehemently.

"Hey," he said, reaching over to grab my hand. "You didn't know, okay? No one blames you for what happened, and Kalen made his own choice to get involved with Breena." He paused for a second and looked around the room. "Do you want some wine? It'll probably make your shoulder feel better."

Breathing a sigh of relief, I smiled and said, "That would be wonderful. I could really use it right now."

Drake left to fetch two glasses and a bottle of the most precious substance in all of the Land of the Fae … faerie wine. Once the bubbly, blue substance landed in my glass I took it and downed it in one gulp. "Be careful, Sorcha. I don't want you getting drunk and taking advantage of me."

"I think you got that backward, genius. Besides, why do I get the feeling you'd like that?"

He smirked seductively and shrugged his shoulder. We ate in silence, staring at each other the whole time. His mouth moved gracefully as he chewed his food, and I sat there mesmerized. Having him in my dreams was one thing, but being with him in person was another. Drake cleaned our empty plates off the table and took my hand, lifting me up. We walked down the hallway, hand in hand, until we reached his bedroom door.

When he opened it, I was amazed to see an elegant yet masculine set up. Everything was laid out in blues and gold. Blue was his favorite color and also the one color he loved seeing me in. Running my hands along his bed, I got a sudden jolt of jealousy thinking he'd probably had numerous women in that very room.

"How many women have you had in here?" I asked bluntly.

Drake came up behind me and wrapped his arms around me. "None," he answered gruffly in my ear. "Only you."

"You expect me to believe that?" I replied, turning around to face him.

"It's the truth," he admitted. "I've had other women, just like you have had other men, but never in this room, never in my personal space."

Curiosity got the better of me, so I decided to ask

the question I was too scared to ask him before, for fear of the answer. "Were you seeing someone during the time of our dreams?"

He narrowed his eyes at me, but I stood my ground and kept eye contact, determined to take the answer with dignity. Thankfully, after only a few seconds he shook his head. "No, I was not seeing anyone. Once I met you I couldn't think of anyone else, and once the dreams started ..."

Releasing my held breath, I smiled. "Yeah, I know what you mean."

"What about you?" Drake asked darkly. I could hear the jealousy in his tone because I knew what he was asking. "Weren't you seeing Alston at the time? You never dreamed about me with him in your bed did you?"

"No!" I shrieked. "The night of the Winter Ball was when I called it off with him. I knew then that my heart was taken even if I didn't want to admit it."

Drake smiled and ran his hands through my hair. "You are so beautiful," he whispered. "I want to make love to you tonight."

His words made my heart stop in my chest, and my core to clench with need. I wanted him too, but there could be consequences to our actions if we sealed our bond. "We don't know if I'll be able to open the magic box to get the scroll out, Drake. I want to feel you inside me more than anything, but I have to know that my pure blood will get that scroll out."

He nodded, but there was a gleam in his eye. "I know, and I understand, but that doesn't mean we can't enjoy ourselves together and finish what we started in our dreams?"

Smiling devilishly at him, I no longer wanted to waste time and began to take off my clothes. "You are one sneaky bastard, Drake."

Once my clothes were discarded, I helped Drake loosen his. I ran my hands over his warm skin while he did the same to me, the sound of our labored breathing the only noise in the room. In one quick move, he lifted me up and placed me on the bed. He kissed me fiercely, trailing his hand down my cheek, down my neck, until he settled on my breast. His thumb padded over my nipple, making it hard and puckered while he massaged my breast. He groaned deep in his chest and moved down to lick my sensitive breast, sucking generously … tenderly. Arching my back, he wrapped his arms around me, pulling me closer before settling me back down. My core was wet and ready for the taking, but I knew we couldn't finish.

Slowly and deftly, Drake entered me with his long fingers, thrusting them in and out. His tongue was hot and greedy, exploring my body, and on top of the friction his hand was bestowing upon me, I'd almost lost all control.

"I need to be inside you," Drake growled.

Breathless, I sighed, "Please don't say that, Drake. I want you too much right now."

"Dammit, Sorcha, I can feel you getting tighter," he breathed. "You're going to make *me* lose control."

His words and the sound of his voice was enough to make me want to orgasm. Reaching between our bodies, I trailed my fingers down his long, hard cock before surrounding it with my hand. He jerked once and let out a shaky breath. "I can't let you have all the fun, can I?" I asked, sounding husky and animalistic.

At a hard and steady pace, I moved up and down his cock, enjoying the moans that escaped his lips. His rhythm matched mine as we both pleasured each other. Only when I felt his rigidness grow harder did I let myself give in.

"Oh … Drake!" I screamed, my back arching off the bed.

"Sorcha … Ah!"

My body jolted as the orgasm sent shock waves through every limb of my being. Drake collapsed beside me, breathing heavy and holding me tight. I snuggled into his warmth, and placed my head on his chest where his heart was beating uncontrollably. He was mine, and I was his. The day couldn't come soon enough for us to be able to seal our bond.

"I love you, Sorcha. I know it may be soon, but in all reality we've been together for a while now. I can't deny what's in my heart any longer, and I don't want to. You're mine, and I'm going to make it rightfully so the moment we come back from this journey."

"I like the sound of that, and just so you know, I fell in love with you from the very beginning. I also hated you at times, but that's because you were more arrogant back then."

He laughed and kissed me deeply, making my core tighten again. "I think I need a shower ... a cold one," he admitted sheepishly, looking down between his legs where his cock lay hard against his stomach.

"You are insatiable," I moaned.

"Only for you, beautiful."

We got out of bed and climbed in the shower together. He worked his hands all over my body, cleansing me with soap just as I did with him, both of us lingering on certain areas of our bodies. After the shower, I dressed in one of his T-shirts while he climbed into the bed naked.

"You're killing me, Drake. How am I supposed to sleep beside you like that?" I asked, placing my hands on my hips.

He smiled. "Get used to it, beautiful. You're going to be sleeping beside me like this for the rest of your life starting tonight. Now come over here."

Drake held his arms out and I happily allowed myself to be folded into his body. He held me tight, breathing against my ear, until he soon relaxed his hold and fell asleep. Closing my eyes, I imagined our dream world and let myself fall into it. In that realm, nothing else mattered except us, and our desires. We made love to each other that night, over and over, until the sun came up the next day. Our journey was about to begin.

Drake and I were planning to leave as soon as possible. The longer we waited, the more time for things to fail. I was packing a light bag when Oren entered the room. "Why do you need a guardian, *ai dulin*? It seems you never need me."

"Oh, Oren," I said, turning around. I walked over to him and cupped his face in my hands. "I will always need you. You know me better than anyone, and there's no one else that can put up with all my bullshit."

"Then let me come with you," he insisted.

"No!" I replied forcefully. "I've seen the way Calista looks without her guardian, and I don't want that emptiness inside of me. She misses Merrick, and every time she sees you or Meliantha's guardian, Ashur, she's reminded of what she lost. I'm not as strong as her, Oren."

Oren wrapped his arms around my waist and

hugged me tight. We usually didn't show a lot of physical affection, but maybe the Summer heat was melting him a bit. When he released me, he looked down at my newly changed skin. "I must say, you look stunning like this. No more tanning beds for you?" He laughed, while I scowled.

Ryder and Kalen used to give me hell when I came back burnt like a lobster from experimenting with a tanning bed one time in the mortal realm. I was red for a week, but then right back to being pale the next. It was an experience from hell, and one I'd never forgotten.

"It's strange to think that we're both going to be Summer Fae," I said thoughtfully.

Oren winked and nudged me in the side. "Who says I'm going to follow you to your new court?"

"You better be!"

We both laughed, and once my bag was packed, Oren walked me down to Drake who was waiting patiently by the palace doors. After kissing Oren on the cheek, I whispered in his ear, "Please say good-bye to Sarette for me."

He nodded. "I will. Be careful, *ai dulin*."

"Always," I replied back silently.

When we walked down to the horses I was confused. "Why are we riding horses?" I asked Drake curiously. "Why can't we just fly?"

Drake sighed, strapped my saddle in place, and turned to face me. "I was hoping you wouldn't ask, but since you did I'll tell you. We don't know what's going to happen on this journey, but I want us to be prepared. If something was to happen to me and I couldn't fly, we would have the horses to help us. Also, when I transform from dragon back to myself it wipes out a lot of my energy."

"Then why don't we have others coming with us to help?"

"Because, beautiful, if I needed to transform quickly to get you away from danger, where would that leave my warriors? I wouldn't be able to protect them or get them out safely. It would be sentencing them to death."

He helped me up on my horse, and climbed up on his looking confident and strong. The gold plated armor, along with the sleekness of his body, made him look like a God of War. No wonder everyone was in awe and also afraid of him.

"I understand," I said.

It all made sense after he explained. We had to do this alone, to be quick and stealthy, and to spare the lives of so many others if they were to come with us and danger followed. Drake rode up beside me and pulled me over by the arm until he could reach my lips.

"Last night was amazing," he breathed against my lips. "Let's get this over with so I can claim your body and make you my queen."

His gray eyes slit to that of the dragon, which I'd

grown to realize they did when he felt strongly about something. It was amazing to watch and also intoxicating to know he felt that strongly for me. "Sounds good to me," I replied breathlessly.

We took off at a rapid pace toward the Endelyn Mountains, where the scroll was supposed to be hidden. If everything went smoothly, we should get there by tomorrow and be back by nightfall. We were one step closer.

Chapter Twelve

DRAKE

Watching Sorcha on her horse—the way she rode, the way her sleek black hair billowed out in the wind—made me hard as a rock. No other female has made we want something so bad the way she makes me want her. The magical pull to her didn't help matters either.

We laughed and raced for hours until the terrain grew too wooded and bumpy to continue at that fast pace. It also helped give the horses a break. "You're really competitive. It's one of the things I love about you," I said to her.

She laughed. "Yeah, you should know about that. Don't you remember how angry I'd get when you'd kick my ass when we trained in our dreams?"

Smiling, I remembered our dreams very well. I'd taught her so many new moves and she was an ace at them. "I did that on purpose, you know. You were always so hot when you got angry. It was a warrior's wet dream come true."

Rolling her eyes, she smacked me on the arm. We rode side by side in silence until a noise off to the side had us halting in our tracks. I drew my sword just as Sorcha grabbed her spear. "Someone's out there," I said carefully. The forest was quiet, but I could hear the labored breathing of someone, or something, coming from the thicket. "Wait here," I commanded forcefully. She narrowed her eyes, but nodded. Thankfully, she didn't argue with me.

Climbing off my horse, I headed straight for the overgrown grass of the thicket. Slowly and with my sword drawn, I made my way to what appeared to be a warrior lying on the ground. When the person came into view my eyes grew wide in shock.

"Sorcha!" I yelled.

She jumped off her horse and ran straight to me. When she looked down at the warrior on the ground she screamed in joy. "Alston!" she called out, falling to her knees beside him.

He opened his eyes wearily and settled them on her. "Sorcha?" he responded weakly, pulling her down to the ground and into his arms.

Jealousy instantly flared in my gut watching him touch her, but I clenched my teeth together to keep my mouth shut. I didn't wish the guy to be dead, and I was glad he was alive for Sorcha's sake, but why the hell was he always in the way somehow?

"We thought you were dead! Sarette thinks you're dead! She's been grieving for days," Sorcha said to him.

When his eyes focused on her they instantly grew dark and dangerous. "Well I see *you* hadn't been grieving for me," he spat out.

I was two seconds away from shutting that mouth of his up when Sorcha beat me to it. "Really, Alston? That's what you have to say to me after we find your sorry ass. Get over yourself!" She got up from the ground and came to my side. Alston staggered to his feet, glaring at Sorcha and me. I kept my face blank, but made sure to show some of the smugness I felt.

The tension visibly regressed from Alston's shoulders when he lowered his head, but it looked forced. "I'm sorry," he sighed. "It's been a long couple of days."

"What happened to you?" Sorcha asked. "Why didn't you make your way back?"

"When I got hurt and went down, no one saw me, and when I woke up everyone was gone. With no food or water, I drifted into a haze and wandered around until I ended up here. I wanted to wait until I was perfectly healed before I made my way back. If anyone attacked, I wouldn't have had the strength to fight."

Sorcha nodded in understanding. "Well, I'm glad we found you. Sarette's going to be so happy when you make it home."

Alston furrowed his brows and looked around the forest. "What are you two doing out here by the way?" he asked.

"It's a long story," Sorcha said, glancing at me then back to him. "We need to rest anyway. I know you have to be starving." She turned on her heels and headed back to the horses while Alston fell into step beside her, a little too close.

After we ate our food, Sorcha explained to Alston what all had happened and where we were going. She even told him about us and the changes that were getting ready to happen when we form our own Summer Court. He became visibly angry and stalked off from us. I was glad he didn't pick a fight because I probably would've killed him, and I was glad Sorcha didn't want to follow him because I wasn't going to let her.

"He's pretty volatile," I noticed.

Sorcha sighed. "Yes, he is."

Anger flowed through me as I imagined him taking his anger out on her. What did he do when she broke it off with him? My hands started shaking, and I knew my eyes had changed. Clearly they had because Sorcha looked at me warily. "He didn't hurt you when you two were together, did he? Because if he did, I'm going to kill him now. No one would ever know."

"Drake!" she shrieked. "No, he never hurt me. He got really possessive at times, but he learned quickly he couldn't control me. A few punches and black eyes did the trick."

I laughed, imagining her kicking his ass. "Good," I stated wholeheartedly. "He deserves a good ass kicking now."

"That may be so, but what are we going to do about him? Are we taking him back or is he coming with us?"

I groaned. "As much as I want him to go home, we just don't have the time for it. If the dark sorcerer comes back and knows what we're up to, he'll be on our trail or he'll get to the scroll first and put it somewhere else. So, unfortunately, he stays with us."

As if my words called him forth, Alston came through the shadows of the forest and sat down by the fire. "It's getting late. We probably should get some sleep and continue on in the morning," I insisted.

Sorcha stretched out her glorious body, and cuddled up next to me not even acknowledging Alston's presence. Alston scowled as she kissed me on the lips and fell asleep instantly in my arms. Once she was completely out, I turned my attention to Alston and stared daggers at him. "I'd appreciate it if you kept your hands to yourself from now on," I warned him.

Alston's eyes grew smug. "What's wrong? Jealous?"

"Hardly," I stormed back. "She's with me now, and a future queen of the Summer Court. You may still love her, or want her, but it's over. Show some respect and back the fuck off."

"See … that's the thing," Alston sneered. "I have no respect."

With that, he turned his back to me and lay down on the ground, clearly saying the conversation was over. It was far from over, and I was going to make sure he fully understood that.

When I fell asleep, Sorcha was waiting for me.

"What took you so long?" she asked curiously.

"Oh, you know …" I began sarcastically. "Just warning Alston to keep his distance, but of course, he challenged me."

Sorcha shook her head. "I told you, he's possessive. He said he was going to work on it, but obviously, I guess he's not getting the picture."

"He's not welcome in our court, Sorcha," I added forcefully. "Sarette is your friend, and if she decides to follow you that's great, but she has to know he can't come."

Sorcha nodded in agreement. "I understand, and I agree with you. Maybe he'll come to his senses when I'm gone for good, when our bond is complete."

"He has no choice but to let you go, beautiful. If

he causes a problem I'm going to have to deal with it my way. He's not going to disrespect me or you by acting this way."

Sorcha smiled and placed her finger to my lips. "Please tell me we aren't going to talk about Alston this whole time. Our dreams are about me and you. What adventures are we going to go on tonight?"

"We could visit your home in the Winter Court," I suggested. "I know you miss it."

She shrugged and said thoughtfully, "I will miss it, and once we get back I'll have to face my parents. They're going to be so angry with me when they find out what I'm doing."

Taking her in my arms, I held her tight. "You'll be safe with me. I'll make sure you get back all in one piece."

Running her hands along my back, she whispered against my chest, "I know, Drake, but tonight I want to feel safe in our court. Let's picture it together and go there. I want to feel like I'm at home."

"Home," I repeated, smiling.

Closing our eyes, we both envisioned our court the way we wanted it to be: white, sandy beaches, clear blue water, palm trees, salty sea air, and us right in the middle of it. Even in the dream I felt at home, truly and utterly at home.

The next morning came quickly, and once the sun was up we packed our supplies and began our journey. Since we only had two horses, Alston rode Sorcha's horse while she and I rode on mine. The ride was quiet until Alston opened his smart ass mouth.

"I don't see why you don't just fly while Sorcha and I ride the horses. You're weighing yours down with both your weights. I'm starting to feel sorry for it."

Growling, I turned to face him with my lethal gaze. "My horse will be perfectly fine, and besides, I'm not stupid enough to leave her alone with you."

"She's been alone with me many times and I've never heard her complain," he taunted suggestively.

Sorcha tensed in front of me, and glared at Alston, fuming. "Enough!" she yelled. "What the hell is the matter with you? I thought you said you were going to change. What happened to that?"

"I'm trying," he yelled back. "It's hard to see you two all over each other when I'm still in love with you. I'm sorry if you don't understand that."

Sorcha paused and stared at him for a tense moment. She released a shaky breath and continued,

"I know you still love me, but the snide remarks need to stop. If you have a problem with me and Drake being together you're going to have to get over it. No one is making you stay with us. I'm sure you can find the way back to the Winter Court."

"I'm not leaving you," he answered firmly. "I don't think I can."

My anger grew with every word he said, and no matter what Sorcha believed, Alston was definitely going to be a problem. Sorcha tilted her head back to me and said, "Pull the reins. We need to stop." I did as she said and we came to a halt.

When Alston's horse stopped, she glared at him and began, "Alston, I *will* be leaving soon. I'm not going back to the Winter Court. It's not my home anymore."

"Well, then I'll follow you to Summer," he promised.

When I opened my mouth to protest, Sorcha jabbed me in the leg and whispered, "Let me handle this." Biting my tongue, I kept my mouth shut even though I was shaking furiously.

"You can't follow me, Alston. You don't belong in Summer."

"What about Sarette?" he asked. "She won't leave the Winter Court without me."

Sorcha shrugged her shoulders regretfully. "Then I guess she'll have to stay in Winter."

Alston fumed, his eyes going wide in disbelief.

"Are you serious? You would actually refuse your best friend because of me?"

Her reply was soft and tinged with regret. "I'm sorry, Alston, but I have no other choice. *You've* given me no other choice."

His mouth flew open and he sat there frozen atop the horse. When he made no attempt to move, I spurred our horse on to continue the way. We weren't far from Endelyn because I could see the mountains looming ahead. The tallest peak soared high into the sky above, hidden by the gray clouds. Sorcha shivered as her gaze shot up the expanse of the mountain.

"Wow," she breathed in awe. "I'm so glad we don't have to climb that."

"Me too." I laughed. "Are you ready to go up there?"

"As I'll ever be."

"Okay, first thing I need to do is get out of my clothes and transform. I'll stay in dragon form while we're up there so as soon as you get the box open and grab the scroll we can fly down. After that, I'll change back and we can make our way home."

Sorcha nodded. "All right, let's get this done."

She bounced on her feet like she'd always do before we trained in our dreams. I'd come to realize that was her way to get the adrenaline going. I also thought it might be her trying to hide her nervousness, which she surely hated admitting to.

"Hey," I murmured softly, taking her face in my hands. "You're not alone. I'm going to be there with you, just as a dragon."

Releasing a shaky breath, she sighed. "I know. I think I'm just a bit nervous, and you know how I hate to admit that."

Looking her in the eyes, I kissed her lips long and hard until she relaxed against me. "I love you, Sorcha. You're going to do fine up there."

She smiled and brought her lips to mine again. "Thank you, and I love you, too," she whispered across my lips.

Releasing her from my grasp, I began to strip out of my clothes and initiate the change. "When you're ready and secure, just call out to me and we'll fly."

"I will."

Once the transformation was complete, Sorcha climbed up on my back and settled into position. Her legs were clenched tight, holding her in place, while her hands wrapped firmly into my hair. She felt so light, almost breakable and fragile against my muscular dragon frame, but she was mine to protect, and I would do so with my life.

"I'm ready, Drake!" she called out.

As soon as I heard those words I was off into the sky. My wings flapped hard, lifting us off the ground and smoothly into the air. The wind grew colder and the air grew thinner the further up we went, and it wasn't long before we reached the top, concealed by the clouds. We made it to the top, now it was time for the search.

Chapter Thirteen

Sorcha

When we reached the top of the mountain, Drake lowered himself to the ground so I could slide down his scaly skin with ease.

"Thank you," I murmured, trailing my gaze over the lonely mountain top.

Even though Drake was there with me as a dragon, I still felt oddly alone knowing he couldn't speak to me. Looking around, there was nothing nice about my surroundings. I could feel the dark magic plaguing the life of the land, making it gloomy and dank. I shivered in response when I felt the darkness float over my skin. There was no life, not even a shred of it as I walked around the huge boulders. It was almost like everything turned to stone ... empty.

"Okay, I need to find the pile of rocks Brokk mentioned. He said I'd be able to feel the dark magic and pinpoint the scroll, but I can feel it everywhere. It's hard to pinpoint it when it's surrounding you. I guess I could always try my earth magic."

Drake nodded his large dragon head in agreement. With my natural ability being with the earth, I decided to give it a try, to see if it would lead me to the scroll. Kneeling on the ground, I placed my hands on the cold, stone pebbles. I concentrated as hard as I could on finding the life inside the mountain. It was there, just deep and buried. I could feel its essence drawing up through the ground until it pooled at my hands and feet. My hands tingled as the power flowed through my body.

"Please … show me the way," I pleaded.

The energy surged beneath my feet and it was as if my legs had a will of their own; one minute I didn't know where to go and the next I was being pulled like a magnetic force. My eyes were closed in concentration as I followed the invisible path in my mind. Once the magic dissipated and the connection broke, I knew I was where I needed to be. When I looked down, there was a collection of rocks piled into a mound just like Brokk had said.

"Drake, I found it!"

He came up behind me and hovered over my shoulder. The heat he gave off was scorching, but what else was there to expect from a fire breathing dragon. He winked at me with his smoky gray eyes as I ran my hands down his snout, smiling.

"Here we go," I began.

Rock after rock, I moved them aside until there were no more. Nothing was underneath the rocks except dirt, so I scooped it away—layer by layer—until I came upon something hard. Smiling, I pulled the box out of its resting place, blew off the dirt, and held it in my hands. It was made of wood, but had symbols carved on all sides, symbols that I had no clue what they meant. My hands hummed with energy, and it wasn't the good energy either. There was only a slight seal where I could see where the box was connected together. I had an idea, and I was going to try it.

"Oh, what the hell," I said, picking up the box. Raising it high over my head, I slammed it down on the rocks as hard as I could. Over and over, I threw it on the ground and rammed it into the rocks hoping it would open, but it never did. There wasn't even a scratch or dent on the surface of that dreaded box.

Drake's dragon eyes showed amusement as he sat there watching me, almost as if he was laughing at me. "Hey, it was worth a shot," I told him. "I'm sure you would've tried the same thing."

Placing the box on a nearby rock, I wiped my sweaty hands on my black, leather pants, and realized that soon my silver and black armor would be traded in for the gold and brown of Summer. All I needed was to get the scroll and go home, but first, I had to pay the price; the price to save my people. By offering my blood, I was willingly giving the dark sorcerer my power, and willingly making him stronger. It sickened me to know that after this he was going to have *my* power coursing through his veins. I felt violated even though this was my decision, and my choice to have my power taken.

Closing my eyes, I took a few deep breaths. Drake nudged me in the side and made a small whimpering sound. He hated that I had to do this. "I'm okay, Drake. It just pisses me off that when I do this the dark sorcerer will have won another round. I wanted to be different, to be the one he couldn't get, but that's not going to happen. Instead, I'm offering myself up on a golden platter. I just hate that whatever we do, he has a way to change it and make us look like the fools."

Drake growled in response, and I could tell in his dragon eyes that he agreed and understood. I knew Drake was in there, but it still amazed me how a dragon, dangerous and lethal, could have love and understanding in its eyes.

"Okay, here I go."

Not wanting to waste any more time, I pulled my spear out from the harness on my back. The spear point was sharp; a light scraping of the blade could drag deep down to the bone if too much pressure was applied. Carefully, I ran my palm over the sharp edge, instantly drawing a stream of blood. I placed my hand over the box and let the blood flow freely. It coated the outer edge and slowly ran down the sides of the wood. Nothing was happening.

"I wonder how much blood it needs," I mumbled

to myself and Drake.

I took the spear and sliced open my other hand, hoping the extra blood would get it going. The pool of blood surrounding the box had me shaky, and staggering to stay on my feet. Blood didn't bother me, but the amount I was losing did. Drake hissed and began looking angry. He wanted me to stop, but I knew I had to keep going.

"Just … a … little … more," I sputtered weakly.

My vision began to blur and I struggled to stay on my feet. My legs gave out from beneath me and I collapsed onto the ground. I clenched my hands into tight fists to stop the flow of blood. Falling on my back, I closed my eyes, feeling too weak to move. When I glanced up, Drake was staring at the box in awe. *Was it working*? I wondered. I sat up slowly, and I was amazed to see that the box was now glowing and lifting into the air. Getting shakily to my feet, I brought up my hands and lightly placed them on both sides of the floating box. The lid started to open, and a bright flash of light burst from the inside, momentarily blinding me.

When my vision cleared I saw the scroll, the one piece of paper that could help save my land. It was a thick, yellow piece of parchment rolled into a cylinder with a ribbon wrapped around it. My heart thundered desperately in my chest, and it was telling me to grab the scroll and run as fast as I could. I took it out of the box and slowly unrolled it, not wanting to jeopardize the paper in any way. There were so many ancient symbols and texts that it was confusing to read. I could make out some of it, but I knew there was only one person who could decipher the full meaning … Elvena. We needed to get to her quickly.

I put the scroll in my leather pouch that was secured to my armor belt. If I closed it in the box again I took the chance of it sealing and never getting it out. I didn't want to do that. Drake was waiting patiently for me so I staggered over to him and climbed up on his back.

"I'm ready to go!" I called out to him.

Holding the box securely in my hand, I held onto Drake with the other. My palms ached, but the bleeding had finally stopped. Drake flew off the mountain and into the wind, heading straight down to the valley below where we left the horse. If I wasn't so drained I'd find the flight exhilarating, but hopefully within the next hour I'd have my strength back. It took a lot of blood to open that damn box.

When Drake landed and I slid off his back, he immediately changed back. He was naked, but it didn't stop him from scooping me into his arms. "Are you okay?" he asked, sounding worried, running his hands over my body.

"I am now," I said, smiling weakly.

He laughed and kissed my lips before fetching the clothes he left by the horse. After his clothes were put on, he hastily took me in his arms again. "I was so worried about you up there," he whispered in my ear while breathing me in. "I wasn't going to be too happy if you'd let yourself bleed out. I was two seconds away from knocking you out."

"You wouldn't dare, and anyway, I'm fine now." I pulled back and tucked the box under my arm. "Let's go home."

"Not so fast," a cold, dark voice echoed behind us.

Drake and I both stiffened and turned around slowly to see a man standing casually behind us. At first glance he looked almost angelic, but it didn't take long to know he was anything but that. His shoulder-length brown hair was shiny and straight, and the features of his face were sharp, but yet ethereal. How could someone so evil look the way he does? He was the epitome of a beautiful man, but the eyes … the eyes gave him away along with the black aura surrounding his body. His dark gaze was alight with extreme power, and it didn't take long to recognize it as mine.

"Alasdair," I whispered.

He closed his eyes and groaned. "Hmm, hearing my name cross your lips makes me think naughty things, Princess. But look at you, and how you've changed. I think you two have been doing some naughty things, am I right?"

"What the …" Drake started and lunged, but my grip on his arm kept him in place.

The dark sorcerer waggled his finger at Drake. "You have nothing to worry about, dragon. I don't want your princess. Although, I must say those Winter women definitely know how to fuck," he said, looking at me and licking his lips. "I believe I've been that route once before with your friend, Breena, if I'm not mistaken. Right, Princess?"

Ignoring the last question, I got down to business. He was goading me and I wasn't going to give in. "What do you want, sorcerer?" I asked vehemently, even though I already knew the answer.

His smile disappeared. "Don't play dumb with me, Princess. Hand over the box," he ordered.

Drake grabbed my arm. "Don't," he hissed in my ear.

Never taking my eyes off of the sorcerer, I whispered lightly so only he could hear me. "It's okay. Trust me." Slowly, I trudged over to the sorcerer and reluctantly handed over the box, making sure not to touch his hands. I didn't want to touch pure evil.

"Well, that was easy." He smiled, but then narrowed his eyes at me. "But an empty box is *not* what I want. I want the scroll."

"How do you know it's not in there?" I asked.

He stared at me blandly and held out his hand. "You wouldn't have handed over the box so easily. Now give it to me!" His eyes shifted to Drake, who had started slowly moving away from me, preparing

151

to do to something heroic no doubt, but the sorcerer caught onto it.

"And before you decide to do something stupid …" Instead of finishing his sentence, he caught us both off guard by grabbing me in a lightning fast move. He now had me trapped in his arms with a vial of something liquid and obviously lethal close to my lips. I struggled against his hold, but his grip tightened, keeping me caged against his body while he tormented me.

He ran his nose through my hair and moaned while trailing one of his hands over my breasts, down to my hip, and finally to the inside of my thigh. "Fuck, you smell so good … just like Summer. It brings back a lot of memories."

"Ugh, you make me sick," I hissed. Reaching into my leather pouch, I sifted through it quickly until I found what I needed, and held up the scroll so he could see it. "Dammit, here's your scroll! Now let me go! I'd rather die than be touched by you again."

Drake shook with fury, but before he could charge, someone yelled out from behind the trees. It was Alston! "What the hell do you think you're doing?" he demanded.

"Ah, well if it isn't the scorned lover come to rescue the day," Alasdair teased. "Or is he, might I ask?" He tilted his head so he could address Alston. "You have nothing to worry about, she's all yours." Startled, I gasped and he continued gleefully, "That's right, Princess. You didn't know your ex-lover schemed behind your back, did you? I was shocked when he came to me. Most people want power in return for fealty, but not this one. Oh no, he wanted you, and now I'm going to give you to him."

"What?" I screamed, at the same time Drake yelled, "Like hell you are!"

"I'm afraid you don't have a choice, young Prince. Because once I force this concoction down Sorcha's throat she's going to forget all about you. You'll be nothing to her. She'll only know of her life in the Winter Court before you ever came into her life."

Wide-eyed, my heart hammered in my chest as I stared at Drake, who tried to hide his panic. "You lie!" he yelled half-heartedly. "She'll never be able to forget about me. I'm in her blood, and no matter where I have to go or what I have to do I'll always find her and bring her back."

"Not this time I'm afraid," the dark sorcerer bragged.

My heart hammered in my chest and my mind was reeling. I could feel Alasdair's emotions through touching him and everything was so jumbled together, but the main emotion I felt was doubt. What did he doubt? I tried to concentrate on finding the truth of it, but his grip was bruising and constricting as he held me to him. I could barely breathe much less think. Gasping, I clawed and struggled in his arms.

Grunting with trying to keep his hold on me, the dark sorcerer growled in my ear, "You're a feisty thing, aren't you? I think our Alston is going to have his hands full. All right, it's time to say good-bye to your prince, my sweet vixen."

"Drake!" I yelled. The moment I opened my mouth, the dark sorcerer forced the hot, silvery liquid down my throat. Choking, I tried to spit out as much as I could, but it was too late. So many things happened at once. Drake lunged for me, but I was quickly thrown into Alston's arms and whirled backwards. The world began to spin as I was whisked away from Drake, away from my life, and away from my memories.

I remembered screaming Drake's name, and watching in slow motion as he tried to grab me before all went black, and before I lost ... myself.

Chapter Fourteen

"Sorcha!" In the blink of an eye she was gone, taken from me as I stood there helpless.

The dark sorcerer's laugh echoed in my ear as I turned around to face him. "Oh, don't look so sad, little Prince. At least she's alive," he taunted jokingly.

"Where is she?" I demanded, pulling my sword and advancing on him.

"Oh, I'd say she's in Alston's arms in the mortal realm somewhere. Who knows really? I didn't care to ask."

"You son of a bitch! I *will* find her," I swore wholeheartedly. I was only a few steps away, sword in hand, when the dark sorcerer slowly turned into his undefeatable shadowy self.

"Good luck with that. Tell Ariella that I'll be waiting for her. I have so many great things planned for her and me."

"Coward!" I yelled, as he vanished into the shadows of the forest.

"Fuck! Fuck! Fuck!" I screamed at myself. Stripping out of my clothes, I had no choice but to transform and fly back to the Summer Court. Usually, I couldn't change back so quickly after turning into the dragon, but with the anger coursing through my body I knew that it'd be easy. Sure enough I felt the change begin as soon as I concentrated on it. When my wings unfurled from my back, I was off. I couldn't think of anything except finding Sorcha.

When the Summer Palace came into view, I bellowed out an ear-splitting wail as I approached. Everyone came running out of the palace, hollering and jumping up and down in excitement. Little did they know how I failed and that I was alone. Once I came into view and they saw I was alone, everyone grew panicked ... Oren especially.

Landing, I changed back immediately and Finn, my second in command, brought over a robe to drape over my shoulders. At that point, modesty was the least of my concern, only Sorcha was.

"Where is she?" Oren yelled. "I can't hear her. What the hell is going on?"

The exertion of the flight had me exhausted and I could barely catch my breath enough to speak. "She's been taken," I growled with anger, anger at myself.

Everyone gasped and put their hands over their mouths in shock. My father, King Oberon, spoke up. "Everyone inside, we can't do this out here."

Hastily, everyone congregated in the throne room

waiting for the details of our botched mission. Finn brought me a set of clothes so I could change out of the robe. Dressing quickly, I took a deep, steady breath before explaining my failure. I glanced at Oren out of the corner of my eye and his whole body shook with pent up rage. He was scowling at me, and I knew that any moment he was going to explode. I didn't know what a guardian bond felt like, but I could assume it was just as great as my bond with Sorcha … strong.

"Everything went fine until it came time to head home. The scroll was in our grasp, but the dark sorcerer intercepted us." Murmurs and shouts erupted from the crowd. Some saying it was a fool's errand while others argued that it had to be done.

"Quiet!" I hollered, my voice booming through the room. "We don't have much time. Anyway, the dark sorcerer appeared and apprehended Sorcha. He took the scroll and forced some kind of memory erasing potion down her throat. So now she's in the mortal realm without any memory of me in her life whatsoever."

The expressions were grave, and for a moment I felt hopeless until a voice spoke out behind me. "Forgive me, Your Highness." I turned to see Grayce, our healer, step forward. "May I have permission to speak?" he asked. My father and I both nodded, so he continued to step forward. "When it comes to the infamous Four princesses, I've learned that not all things go as planned with them. They're strong, and even though some magic works against them, I know it wouldn't be enough to deter them."

"What are you saying, Grayce?" I asked, confused. "That maybe the potion didn't work?"

He shrugged. "I'm pretty sure it worked, especially since she's in the mortal realm. We are all weaker in that world, but I know Sorcha's spirit. If anything, the potion will only be temporary."

Relief flowed through me, but until it wore off she was still susceptible to Alston's advances and the dangers of being around him. If she got her memories back before I found her there was no telling what he would do to her.

"How do you know she's in the mortal realm, son?" my father asked.

"Because he told me, and it makes perfect sense. You see, once Sorcha gave her blood, the dark sorcerer had instant access to her power. He didn't need her anymore, but someone else did, someone that turned against us," I said, peering over at Oren. Sarette was by his side, standing frozen in horror. Her wish to have her cousin alive was about to come true, but he was also dead once I found him.

When I glanced back at my father, his brows were furrowed in confusion. "Who else was there that would want to take her, son?"

"Alston of the Winter Court took her. We thought he was dead after the battle, but he wasn't.

He was hiding out in the woods when Sorcha and I found him. He made a deal with the sorcerer, and in return he took her to the mortal realm so she couldn't be found. With the memories of me and everything that's happened erased out of her mind, he could feed her lie after lie and she wouldn't know the truth."

Sarette's high-pitched wail caught everyone's attention. "He wouldn't do that! He would never betray our court!" I knew it had to be hard to find out that a close family member was a traitor, but at the moment, I couldn't bring myself to feel sympathy for her.

"Be that as it may," I snapped at her. "Your cousin is indeed alive, and he *did* betray your court, the whole Land of the Fae as a matter of fact. He has Sorcha in the mortal realm, and there's no telling what's going to happen to her if we don't find her."

Oren tried to console her, but she pulled away from him and ran out of the throne room. Oren then began to speak, "I know Alston, and I know his ways. If she's lost her memories he's going to manipulate her into thinking something else, and whatever it is, he's going to make it seem like she can't come home. If he steps back in the Land of the Fae he knows he's dead. This was the perfect way to get Sorcha and disappear for good. His obsession with her is lethal. He'll do anything to keep her to himself."

"Where would he take her?" I asked impatiently.

Oren shrugged helplessly. "There are so many

places they used to go together. It could be anywhere, but I have some good guesses."

"Well, then that's where we'll start. We leave immediately, Guardian," I commanded. "I'm not going to stop until I find her."

"Neither am I," Oren agreed, coming to my side.

Oren and I both turned to leave, but stopped when we heard the one question I dreaded someone asking. "How are we going to defeat the dark sorcerer now without the scroll?" Finn asked.

My father sighed, eyed me wearily, and frowned. "We will find another way. There has to be another way." I knew my father didn't believe it, but we still had to make sure our people knew there was hope. I could only pray there was another way to defeat the sorcerer.

Dressed in regular clothes, Oren and I were ready to begin our search in the mortal realm. "How long do you think it'll take Sorcha to get her memories back?" Oren asked.

I shrugged. "I don't know, but we'll find a way to help her. So, where are we going to look first?" I asked him.

Instead of answering, he began forming the portal. When he was done, he stepped through and I followed him into the bustling streets of Paris. "Really, Oren?" I questioned doubtfully. "I didn't take Alston for the romantic type."

Oren grunted. "He wasn't. He just tried to make Sorcha think he was. He was so desperate for her attention that he brought her here, and other places, in hopes she would fall in love with him."

"Did it ever work?"

Oren shook his head. "Not really. For a time, I think she was in love with him, but once she met you she started to pull away from him. He didn't like it and started trying to hold on to her harder. Sorcha isn't the type to be claimed by any man, but in your case I'm sure she'd reconsider. Even now, with you out of her memories, she's still not going to love him like that. However, she *is* going to remember him the way he was before he went possessive on her. They had more of a physical relationship than an emotional one."

Abruptly, I turned to him, growling. "That is the last thing I want to think about right now!"

"I know," Oren agreed calmly. "But if she still thinks they're lovers, then you need to be prepared for what we might find. We don't know how their relationship is going be out here."

Not thinking clearly, I punched the side of the

building we were passing in frustration. I only wished it was Alston's face. Part of the building crumbled on impact, leaving a huge dent in the side. Wide-eyed, I looked around at the people who stopped to stare at me.

"We might need to go or I'm going to get arrested and put in a lab."

Oren agreed. "Good idea. Next time, don't try to knock down a building. We're trying to be discreet, and anyway, I don't sense Sorcha here at all."

"Neither do I," I mumbled wearily. Once we got into a deserted alleyway, Oren made another portal. "Where to this time?" I asked.

Oren sighed and answered, "To another one of Alston's many places he liked to lure in Sorcha."

"Great," I muttered sarcastically. "Remind me never to visit any of them with her when I get her back."

"You have my word, Your Highness."

We stepped through yet another portal, knowing it was going to be one of many. Desperate couldn't even begin to describe the way I was feeling.

Chapter Fifteen

The bed was soft underneath my body, and the sheets were warm against my bare skin. When I tried to turn, I was held in place by an arm across my stomach. Tilting my head back, I could see it was Alston holding me tight, and he was sound asleep. What I didn't understand was why I had no idea where I was or how I got there. By the smells and the feel of the land we were in the mortal realm, but the place we were in was never one I'd been to with Alston. Why couldn't I remember how I got there, and why did my head feel so damn fuzzy? I guess I drank too much faerie wine.

When I pulled the covers off of me, that's when my attention peaked. My skin was no longer the pale white of a Winter Fae, but a golden hue of the Summer. "Holy shit," I whispered. Panicking, I grabbed Alston's arm and shook him forcefully. "Alston, wake up! Something's wrong with my skin," I shrieked.

Alston woke with a start and immediately came to attention. When he saw me going frantic, he placed his hands on my face and pulled me down to him. "Shh, it's okay," he said soothingly. "You're safe now. Everything's going to be all right."

A jumble of questions came to my mind and I couldn't stop from spouting them all. "What happened? Why are we here? Where's Oren? And why do I feel so weird?"

Alston sighed and ran his hands through his hair. "Calm down, Sorcha. It's been a rough couple of days, and there's a lot I need to tell you. Some of it's going to come as a shock, but you need to know that you're safe and so is your family."

"What the hell are you talking about?" I asked frantically.

He paused for a few seconds before answering, and when he did I could tell he was very hesitant in telling me. "There was an attack at the palace," he began. When I opened my mouth to speak, he placed a finger to my lips. "I'm going to tell you everything, okay? Just let me finish." After I nodded, he continued, "When the palace was attacked, you and I were walking to your room. When I opened the door there were people there waiting for you. I don't know how they infiltrated the palace, but they did, and they were coming to take you to the dark sorcerer. After I killed them, we left to find your parents and Oren. Oren wanted to be the one to bring you here, but your parents thought it best that he not follow you. The dark sorcerer knows he would never leave your side, so that made him a target. Wherever he is, you would be, but that's not the case now. When you refused to leave, they had one of the healers give you a potion to knock you out, and for some reason your skin changed after you took it. I don't know. They said it would probably go back to normal soon. I brought you here so you couldn't be found so easily. We have to stay hidden for a while until it's safe to go back."

"It's never going to be safe!" I snapped. "How long do they expect me to stay here?"

Alston's sympathetic gaze was answer enough. "As long as it takes," he suggested sheepishly. "We have to wait here until they come get us."

Jumping out of bed, I stomped over to the window. "Where is here exactly?" I asked, pulling open the curtains.

I was met with rolling hills and trees as far as the eye could see, and I had no clue where we were. Alston came up behind me and wrapped his arms around my waist. I loved the feel of them around me, but for some reason it didn't give me comfort right then. "We're somewhere safe, baby. Why don't you lie down and relax."

Giving in, I nodded and headed back over to the bed. "Okay, but what about clothes and food? How are we going to handle it here if we have to stay more than a couple of days?"

"You don't need to worry about any of that. We have all we need here, and then some to last us a year."

"A year!" I shrieked. "I'm not staying in the mortal realm that long. My people need me. I'm not a coward that runs for the hills, Alston, and you know that. If they haven't come to get me in a week, I'm going back myself."

Alston lowered his head and sighed. "I don't want to stay here that long either, but your parents made me take an oath that I wouldn't let you go back until they're ready for you. I'm sorry, baby, but we have to stay in the mortal realm. If I go against my oath they can punish me to death, and your mother is cold enough to do it, too. I, for one, don't want to die, so please don't condemn me to it."

"Dammit!" I hissed "Why would you do that?"

"I would do anything to keep you safe."

Sagging in defeat, I laid down on the bed and groaned. "I know, and I'm sorry. It's just the thought of being here for a long period of time doesn't settle well with me." I paused to examine the room. It was very rustic, but modernly so. Everything felt and looked new, as if no one had ever stepped foot in the house. "Whose house is this anyway? From the looks of outside it doesn't seem like there's much to do around here. We're going to be bored out of our minds."

Alston grinned and placed his arms on both sides

of my body, pinning me to the bed. He leaned down to kiss me, and I allowed it willingly. His tongue entangled with mine, growing more urgent, but the way he tasted was … different. Why did I remember the taste of Summer? *That's strange,* I thought. When Alston pulled away from the kiss, he said, "I wouldn't say we'd get bored. I can think of a million things we could do together here. But to clear things up, this is my place."

Wide-eyed, I pushed him off playfully. "Why didn't you tell me you had a house in the mortal realm?"

He shrugged. "I don't know. I wanted to surprise you with it one day. I thought it would be good for us to get away sometimes and have our own place to stay."

"Does anyone know you have a place here?"

He shook his head. "No one other than your family when I told them. Why, do you like it?" he asked, grinning roguishly.

"I haven't seen much of it yet, but yes I do. Even though we're in hiding, I bet you're happier than hell being alone with me, aren't you?"

He laughed. "Well, I'd be lying if I said no."

I didn't know what it was, but something felt off with him. I couldn't quite pinpoint it. When he noticed me studying him, he shifted nervously. "Why are you staring at me like that?"

"I don't know," I answered. "You just seem …

different. Is it weird to say that you seem glad that we're away from home?"

His grin looked devilish when he smiled at me. "I'm not necessarily glad that we're away from home, but I *am* thankful that you're safe and with me. I have you all to myself." He paused and kissed me quickly on the lips. "Why don't you rest? I'll be downstairs watching what these mortals call television, and later I'll be up here to join you."

Yawning, I nodded. "Sounds good to me. Wake me up if our people send word?"

"I will. Sweet dreams, baby," he said before leaving the room. Once he was gone, I stared around the room in total confusion. My mind felt jumbled and unfocused. What the hell was wrong with me? Surely, it wasn't the potion affecting me that badly, was it?

Resting on the pillow, it wasn't long before I slowly drifted off into a much needed, dream-filled sleep.

The sand underneath my feet squished between my toes as I walked along the shore. The beach

seemed almost familiar, like home in a way, but I knew it wasn't. The water was warm as it lapped around my ankles and calves, guiding me to go further in its depths.

"Oh, why not," I said to myself.

The water pulled me in, welcoming me in its embrace. Even though I knew how to swim, I could feel the water keeping me afloat. It was strange how it seemed to have a mind of its own, almost like it was protecting me. Out of everything that had happened, this was a welcome escape. If I had to be stuck in the mortal realm, my dreams would be the only link to my world, except this beach didn't exist in the Land of the Fae.

The trees behind the sand bank look exotic and fruitful, and I wished I could stay here and explore every inch of it, but I knew the night time wouldn't last that long. The sun overhead soaked in my skin as I floated along the water, and surprisingly it felt normal. Usually, with my Winter skin it would burn and be very uncomfortable, except my body had changed somehow, welcoming the heat. I guess you can make anything comfortable when you're the one controlling the dream.

However, the water churning underneath me was definitely not my doing. The current electrified all around me and began pulling me back to shore. I stopped kicking my legs and let it guide me. Laughing, I teased the water, feeling somewhat ridiculous, "I thought you wanted me to swim. Are you tired of me already?"

My laugh stopped in my throat when I saw someone on the shore waiting for me. When the water guided me to shallow water, I walked the rest of the way out. Glancing around warily, I couldn't help but wonder what was going on.

"Um ... why are you here?" I asked him.

His eyes were unsure and slightly sad as he stared at me. "I think because you brought me here, and I'm hoping like hell I'm right," he answered. His eyes were full of passion and longing, and he was gazing at me as if we were lovers. I laughed out loud, thinking how ridiculous my mind was wandering.

"This is crazy! I have no clue why you'd be here or what you're talking about." I ran my hands over my face. "Oh, I must be losing my mind."

He moved closer, as if not to startle me, like I was a lion ready to flee. "You need to let me explain. I know what you are, Sorcha, and this dream is one of many that we've shared together."

"No," I laughed, exasperated. "I think I'd remember if I'd been dreaming about the infamous Drake. It's kind of hard not to miss the flaming red hair and smoky eyes, and not to mention, I've never even actually talked to you before." Closing my eyes, I said to myself, "This is a really weird dream. When I open my eyes, he'll be gone."

I counted to ten with my eyes closed and when I

opened them, he was gone. That was until he came up behind me and wrapped me in his arms, tight. "What the hell are you doing? Get off me!" I snapped, struggling half-heartedly in his grip. In a way I didn't really want to fight him off because I couldn't deny that it felt like I belonged in his arms.

Grunting with trying to keep me still, he whispered in my ear, "I'm only doing this to see if it helps. Otherwise, I don't think you'd let me touch you. Feel me, Sorcha, breathe me in and tell me you don't know who I am on the inside. I have to believe you'll remember me when I find you." He ran his hands along my bare arms, making me shiver. "Look at your skin, it reflects my own because once you gave yourself over to me you changed. This land you brought us to is ... or will be, our home once I get you back. I will find you, and that is a promise."

I couldn't stop myself from breathing him in if I tried. His scent was so familiar, and it only took a second to realize that my body gave off the similar smell of Summer. Why did it do that? Drake slowly released me from his arms, but I stood there frozen and confused like a statue.

"I don't understand," I muttered under my breath, gazing down at my golden skin. "I was too tired to notice when I was awake, but I honestly don't feel like a Winter Fae anymore. Alston said my skin changed after I took the potion."

Turning around, I noticed Drake clenching his

*jaw, and I could feel the fury radiating off of him.
"That was all a lie, Sorcha. Alston is the one who
took you away from me, away from your family. The
potion he speaks of was forced down your throat by
the dark sorcerer. That was the deal he made with
Alasdair. He traded his fealty to your court in return
for erasing your memories of me and our time
together so he could take you away."*

*Exasperated, I said, "This is crazy. Alston would
never do that to me. This is just a dream from all the
stress I've been through." I turned my back on him
and began walking back to the water. "I seriously
think I just lost my mind."*

*I didn't hear Drake approach, but in the blink of
an eye he had me by the shoulders, turning me
around to face him. The electric shock from his touch
made my heart flutter rapidly in my chest, and my
knees go weak. I never in my life had that sort of
reaction to a man, not even Alston. Drake's stormy
gray eyes never wavered from mine, and for the life of
me I couldn't look away. His gaze dropped hungrily
to my lips before descending and closing the gap
between our bodies. He kissed me greedily, and my
body helplessly complied. His hands cupped my face,
holding me there, while he devoured my lips with his
frantic kisses. Even if nothing made sense, there's no
harm in getting a little lip action in my dream. After
all, it couldn't be real.*

When he pulled back, he studied my face. "Do

you remember me yet?" When I shook my head, he groaned and continued, "I'm sorry, Sorcha, but Alston did *turn on your people and take you away. Your family is desperate to get you back; I'm desperate to get you back. Please tell me where you are in the mortal realm."*

I shrugged. "I couldn't tell you that even if I wanted to because I have no clue. We're in a house somewhere in the middle of nowhere."

He visibly deflated and closed his eyes. For some reason I wanted to console him, to tell him I'm all right, but I chose not to. "What has Alston told you?" Drake asked.

"He told me there was an attack at the palace and that my parents told him to take me to the mortal realm so the dark sorcerer couldn't find me. We're supposed to stay there until my family comes for me or sends word."

Drake huffed and paced along the shoreline. "They're not going to find you because they have no clue where you are!" he shouted. He took a few breaths before asking, "What's the last thing you remember?"

Closing my eyes, I concentrated on the last thing that came to my mind. "I remember picking out my dress for the Winter Solstice Ball with Sarette, and watching all the people in my court dance around preparing for the party."

"Let me guess," Drake started, "You picked a

blue evening gown for the occasion, and you wore the crystal necklace your mother gave you for your sixteenth birthday. I remember your dress dipping low in the front, exposing the tops of those beautiful breasts of yours. Anger couldn't begin to describe how I felt when I watched every man ogle you from afar. I do know this though, I was mesmerized the first moment I saw you."

I opened my mouth to speak, but closed it only to do it again. No one has ever said anything like that to me. Curiously, I asked, "If what you say is true about my memories, how long has it been since the Winter Ball?"

His reply was instant, and without hesitation. "It was ten months ago, and after that you visited my dreams every night." I swallowed thickly and glared at him for any sign that he could be lying. His words seemed sincere.

"Are we lovers in these dreams of yours?" I asked, still doubtful. I just don't know if I can believe this. It's not exactly farfetched, but it would be a suicide mission for Alston if he did what Drake said he did.

Drake took my hand and gazed into my eyes. "We're so much more than lovers in our dreams, Sorcha. You're going to be my queen, a leader of the Summer Court. You can already see the change to your body. If there's anything you take from this dream, let it be this ... please, under no

*circumstances trust Alston or let him touch you.
You're mine, and I can't bear it if he uses you and
takes you to his bed."*

*"Okay," I drawled out. "First off, that's just
weird. I'm not going to discuss my sex life with you,
and second, I'm going to need more proof if you
expect me to believe this stuff you're saying to me.
You knowing about my dress color doesn't prove
anything."*

*Drake's wolfish smile gleamed brightly, showing
off his perfectly straight, white teeth. I'm sure he had
the women in the Summer Court falling all over their
feet for him. "You want proof, I'll give it to you. One,
you secretly play the harp, and by the way, I love the
song you wrote for me. You usually play it to lure me
into the dream realm, but since you can't remember it
now it's kind of a moot point." My eyes went wide in
shock and he smiled. Only a couple of people know
about my love of the harp.*

*"Two," he continued, "you love to travel. You
love your home in the Winter Court, but you desire
the chance to see the world, our land and the mortal
one. We spent many of our dreams travelling to exotic
places together, and lastly, I know your guardian
calls you 'ai dulin,' his little bird."*

*Hearing that about my guardian made me want
to believe, but I couldn't seem to wrap my brain
around the truth. Drake took my hands and turned
them palm up, tracing along the gash lines on both*

hands. I never noticed they were there until then. "What are those from?"

He kissed both wounds and said, "These marks are from your unbound courage that you willingly gave up to help save your land. You sacrificed giving your power to the dark sorcerer to get the sacred scroll. You see, we found a way to defeat him, but Alston helped him get away with the scroll after you sacrificed your own blood. You may not believe me, but use your truth seeking abilities on him. Search for it, but do it discreetly. We all fear of what he'll do if he knows you doubt him."

"He would never hurt me."

"He better not," Drake added darkly. "It would only add to the different ways I planned on killing him." The dream realm suddenly shifted, alerting me that our dream was almost over. His eyes widened and he frantically took my face in his hands and kissed me gently. "The dream is about over. You're smart and cunning, Sorcha. Listen to your heart. If you doubt me, and I'm sure you do, go to Oren in your next dream. He will tell you what I say is true."

As my body began to fade out of the dream realm, Drake took me in his arms and whispered in my ear, "I love you, beautiful, and I'm going to find you."

"Sorcha, wake up!" Alston uttered, shaking me by the shoulders.

Groaning, I rolled over. "Leave me alone. I just went to sleep."

"Yeah, about fifteen hours ago," he informed me. "I was getting worried about you."

Rubbing my eyes to clear them, I gazed up into Alston's serious face. The dream slammed into my mind and I tensed, but immediately let it go. "I guess I was tired," I said, yawning.

When he reached up to brush the hair off my face, I latched onto his hand and held it to my face. I had to know for sure if he was telling the truth. "Alston," I murmured, trying hard to concentrate. "Do you think my family will come to get us soon?"

"I don't know, baby, but I'm sure it'll be soon. Until then, we should just enjoy ourselves here." His eyes showed sincerity, but something lacked behind them. What really concerned me was that I couldn't feel any truth from his words ... nothing. It was all blank, like something was blocking me. *Interesting, and not what I was expecting,* I thought.

"Well, let's not worry about all of that right now.

I made you breakfast, and I thought we could explore the land for a while, and then maybe explore this bedroom a little more when we come back. I'm dying to feel those legs wrapped around me." Drake's warning in my dream rang clear in my mind, and my heart lurched with guilt just thinking about Alston and I in bed together. *How was I going to keep my distance until I found out the truth? Could Alston really betray me like that?* I wondered.

"I need to get dressed," I pointed out, hoping it would change the subject.

He grinned and tilted his head toward the closet. "There should be some clothes in the closet for you. Your armor is in there as well, but I don't think that'll be appropriate in this world."

"I would think not," I teased, hoping it didn't sound forced. "Just give me a few minutes to get dressed, and I'll meet you downstairs."

"As you wish, Princess." He kissed me hard against the lips, and before he left the room he looked back once and smiled. My heart ached with doubt, but I knew I only needed to get through the day before night came when I could find Oren. If there was anyone I could trust, it would be him.

Chapter Sixteen

Drake

Before going to sleep the night before, I was pulled in two different directions. I wanted to keep searching for Sorcha, but there was a part of me that wanted to try and sleep to see if Sorcha would come to me. I had a feeling she would, and luckily so, she did even if it was unconsciously done. I jumped out of bed and hastily put on my gear before banging on Oren's door. He answered it in a matter of seconds.

"What happened?" he asked, hopeful. "Did she come to you?"

"Yeah, so get dressed. We have more searching to do."

Ten minutes later we were entering a portal into the mortal realm ... again. "I'm running out of ideas, Your Highness. After these next two stops I'm not going to know where else to look," Oren informed me.

"Let's just hope one of them is where they're at. She's been alone with him now for two days. There's no telling what that bastard is doing with her."

"If you don't mind me asking, what happened in the dream?" Oren asked curiously.

"I told her everything about Alston being involved with the dark sorcerer, and that the potion was what erased her memories. Of course, being the Sorcha we both know and love, she had to question everything and demand proof. I told her some secrets that only she and I shared, and it looked like I might have made some headway with her, but I don't know for sure. She was pretty adamant that Alston would never betray her like that. I told her if she doubted me then she should visit you in her next dream. She trusts you and she knows you would never lie to her."

Oren nodded. "Well, at least it's good news that she called to you in your dreams. It goes to show you that deep down her heart knows who you are."

"Yeah, but she still looked at me as if I was a stranger. Don't you know how hard that was to see her looking at me like that? She at least knows who you are."

"Thank the heavens for that because if she didn't then we'd be in some serious trouble. She trusts me over Alston, which is the good thing. I just hope she comes to me tonight like you suggested, but if she doesn't know where she's at how are we going to find her?" Oren asked.

"Do you think Sarette might know where to find him? They were close after all."

Oren shrugged. "Maybe, but after finding out about his betrayal she's refusing to talk to anyone right now."

I understood her grief, but if she wanted her friend back I was going to need her help. "She's not going to have a choice. If Sarette knows something she *is* going to tell us. One way or another, she's going to tell us where he has her."

Chapter Seventeen

We walked around the land and all we came across were trees, trees, and more trees. We were in complete solitude with no mortal in sight. I wanted to explore further, but Alston insisted we not get too far from the house in case someone came to get us.

"You really picked a place out in the middle of nowhere, didn't you?" I asked as we made our way back to the house.

"It was the safest thing to do," he replied.

"Where are we exactly?" I tried to hide my skepticism, but I could sense he was getting antsy. I glanced at him from the corner of my eye to watch his reaction. Alston had been dodging my questions all afternoon, and wouldn't make eye contact with me when he'd give me his clipped answers.

Narrowing his eyes, he looked over at me curiously. "Why do you keep asking me questions like that? It's like you don't trust me or something."

"It's not that," I lied. "It's just … I can't hear

Oren in my mind, and it's a little unsettling. I've always been able to hear him, even in the mortal realm."

Alston shrugged. "I don't know, maybe your senses were dulled after the potion. I'm sure he's okay." Putting his arm around my shoulder, he leaned down to kiss me on the cheek. "Trust me. You'll be safe with me. I can protect you just as well as he can."

Forcing a smile, I nodded at him, but I couldn't get past the lump in my throat. When we returned to the house, or better yet the empty land where the house should've been, I was deeply confused. Furrowing my brows, I looked around thinking I'd lost my mind. Alston laughed and moved past me.

"It's here, Sorcha. It's just invisible," he told me.

"How?" I asked incredulously. "It takes a lot of power to work a spell like that."

He shrugged, but I could see the tension in his face. "I have my ways," he said quickly. Clearly he didn't want to explain anymore because one minute he was there, and the next minute he disappeared. I was assuming he disappeared through the front door of the house. Unease flowed through my body. I only knew of one person with the kind of magic that could make things appear invisible, and it sure as hell wasn't Alston.

Alston and I fixed dinner together and ate silently. I couldn't ask him anymore questions about the house for fear that he'd get suspicious. It killed me not knowing what was going on. As we sat at the table, Alston watched me with an intensity that had me squirming in my chair, and it wasn't in a good way. It was predatory and possessive, and I felt like I'd seen it before.

Noticing the darkened skies out the window, I turned to Alston and uttered sleepily, "It's getting late, and I'm not feeling too well. I think staying in the mortal realm for so long is starting to wear me down." I didn't wait for a response, but smiled and got up from the table, hoping he wouldn't follow me to the bedroom.

I changed my clothes and breathed a sigh of relief when I came out of the bathroom and noticed I was the only one in the bedroom. Climbing into bed, I rested my head on the pillow and closed my eyes. When I started drifting off, the door to the bedroom opened with a tiny creak of the hinges. I pretended to be asleep when Alston pulled the covers back and crawled into the bed. Silently I groaned, and prayed that he'd keep his distance.

His arm wrapped around my stomach, pulling me tight against him. He nuzzled my hair and took a deep breath in, sighing as he released it. His cock was hard against my back, making me instantly tense. When his hand cupped and began kneading my breast, I shifted so he'd lose his hold.

"Are you avoiding me?" he asked gruffly.

"No, I'm just tired that's all," I replied, trying to sound groggy.

"Uh-huh, why do I not believe you?"

I huffed. "I don't know, maybe because you're thinking with your cock right now."

Growling, he grabbed my arm and pulled me over to face him. His piercing, blue eyes bore into mine with such raw intensity that it had me shivering. "Can you blame me? I've had you to myself for two days and I've been trying to be patient with you, considering all that you've been through, but I need you, baby." He groaned in my ear, pushing his cock against my back so I could feel how much he needed me. "I want to fuck you so bad."

"Not tonight," I mumbled, frustrated.

Alston huffed and got out of bed. I had to find out the truth before I did anything stupid. Once I talked to Oren, things would be clear. When Alston got to the door, he turned back to glance at me. "I'm going to sleep in another room tonight, but you can't keep me waiting long. You're mine, Sorcha, and if—

" He stopped abruptly, clenching his fists. He closed his eyes, as if weighing in his next words. "I just need you, that's all," he sighed, and with that, he opened the door and shut it hard behind him.

After he left, I waited until he closed himself into one of the other rooms before I allowed myself to relax. Sleep started drifting in quickly and once again I was in the dream realm.

The place of choice was my room in the palace back home in the Winter Court. Inside my mind, I concentrated on thinking about nothing except Oren, hoping he would get the pull to join me in the dream. I was starting to doubt Alston, and I needed Oren to back up my doubts before I did something that could jeopardize my family.

When my bedroom door opened, I expected to see Oren, but was met with the glorious sight of Drake instead. Why the hell did I keep dreaming about him? "I didn't call for you," I stated impatiently, even though he was a welcome sight. "I need Oren. I have to know the truth."

He nodded. "I know you do, and it kills me that you can't remember what we are to each other for you to trust me. If you can't get through to him, then you must be in a place where your magic doesn't work."

Narrowing my eyes, I asked, "But how come I can get you here?"

He walked toward me. "Because we have a bond,

Sorcha. It runs a lot deeper than a guardian bond. Nothing could keep us apart."

"What do we do now?" I asked, taking a seat on my bed.

Drake came over and sat beside me, so close that our arms touched. I closed my eyes as the electricity sparked between us and his scent engulfed me. I shivered as thoughts of him taking me on the bed ran through my mind. Stop thinking about that right now, I scolded myself.

"My last option is Sarette. With her being Alston's cousin, I'm sure she'll be able to give us some inclination where he could've taken you."

"Why didn't you think of that before? She should've been the first person to ask," I said, glaring at him incredulously.

His wickedly handsome smile was all I saw as he tucked a strand of hair behind my ear. "And that's what I love about you, beautiful. Your brains with my fierce take on life are going to bring about a lethal Summer Court."

My heart pounded uncontrollably, and watching his smoldering gray eyes take in every inch of me didn't help. Shaking my head, I took in a deep breath. "Just so you know, I'm keeping my distance from Alston for the time being. I'm having concerns of my own, and I'm trying to find out the answers, but he gets tense and short with his replies. I also found out that the house we're in is invisible from the outside."

"Yeah, and I'm sure we all know who did that for him," Drake mumbled.

"I thought that, too. However, I didn't elaborate on the matter since he was already uptight. Alston isn't powerful enough to have that kind of magic, and of course, when I asked him about it he said, 'I have my ways.' What the hell am I going to do if this is all real?"

"It is real, Sorcha. You have all the evidence in front of you. Why can't you see that? This is one situation I wish you weren't so damn stubborn. Anyway, this is kind of what happened to Calista. The house she was in was invisible, and she was also unable to use magic in there. That's most likely why you can't use yours or talk to Oren."

"I don't understand though. Alston and I went for a walk and I still couldn't feel the connection open up to Oren. You don't think he has the whole area placed under a spell, do you?"

He shrugged. "Anything is possible, and it'd make perfect sense."

"Anyway, whatever happens I'm sure I can take care of myself," I said, earning me a smirk from Drake.

"Oh, I know you can take care of yourself. I've trained you in our dreams, except I know you don't remember that right now. I recall you kicking my ass on several occasions."

Laughing, I said, "I'm sure it served you right.

I've always heard you were an arrogant jackass."

He smiled. "Yes, and you were always bold enough to tell me that, too."

It was amazing how easy it was to talk to him. I wondered if he was like this with everyone or just around me. "You know, you're not as bad as I thought you'd be. If this is really how you are and not my imagination then I promise to take back every vile thing I've said about you."

Laughing, he reached for my hand, and I jumped as the electric shock bolted through my body. Drake smiled and ran his fingers over the scar on my palm. "I'm glad to hear it," he sighed warmly. "Just be careful. I know how you are and I know you don't think before you speak sometimes, but do me a favor and don't provoke Alston. If your powers are suppressed, then the only thing you have in your favor is your fighting skills. I know you can take care of yourself, but the real Alston will show his ugly self very soon and you need to be prepared. He's not going to sit idly by. He wants you, and it kills me to know that he's alone with you right now."

"You have nothing to worry about with that. Trust me," I murmured.

"I do with my life."

When the dream world started to fade, I did what I wasn't expecting myself to do. I leaned over and kissed Drake gently on the lips, watching his eyes spring wide in the process. His loving smile was the last thing I saw before he disappeared from my world.

Chapter Eighteen

DRAKE

"Why do you think she couldn't get to me in my dreams?" Oren asked as we walked through the palace in search of Sarette.

"I think the house they're in is enchanted with a spell. I told her in the dream last night that the same thing happened with Calista when she was taken on that first night. The house was invisible, and her magic wouldn't work inside. She seemed to be warming to the idea that Alston isn't who he seems."

"I'm glad she's coming around. Do you think she'll do something stupid when the truth comes out?" Oren asked, even though he knew Sorcha well enough to know the answer. I gave him an incredulous look in response and he sighed, "That's what I was afraid of."

When we reached Sarette's door, Oren knocked. A few minutes passed by and no one answered, so I did the only thing I could think of and barged in. Too much time had wasted, and I refused to give Alston more time with Sorcha. Sarette didn't even budge when Oren and I entered her room. She sat by the window, staring blankly at the gardens below.

Oren walked past me and knelt in front of her. "Sarette? Talk to me," he whispered soothingly to her.

She glanced at Oren briefly before turning back to the window. "My own flesh and blood turned traitor," she cried hoarsely. "How am I going to face everyone back home? They're going to treat me like an outcast now." She put her hands over her face to hide the embarrassment and sobbed uncontrollably.

Oren took her hands away from her face and held them in his. "It wasn't your fault, Sarette. Alston's obsession with Sorcha is what drove him to this insanity. Besides, you don't have to worry about facing everyone at home. You can make a new home in the Summer Court … in Sorcha's Summer Court."

Sarette's eyes grew wide, flicking a nervous glance my way before wiping away her tears. To me she asked, "Would you approve of that, Your Highness? Letting the cousin to a traitor being allowed to live in your court?"

Smiling briefly, I said, "Yes, I would approve, and I know Sorcha will be glad to hear it, too. Nevertheless, we've come for your help."

She stood up slowly, determination in her eyes, and crossed her arms across her chest. "Whatever you need me to do I'll do. I still can't believe Alston would do this. All the lies he told me. I must've been blind not to see the truth."

"Well, Sorcha can't see through it right now either. She's been visiting me unconsciously in her dreams, and she started out not believing anything I said, but I think she's coming around. I've told her secrets that only she and I know of, and she's still skeptical. Are all you Winter women like that? When we get her back I'm going to scold her ass for being so damn stubborn."

"That's her, and unfortunately, she's always been like that. I've just gotten used to it," Sarette laughed half-heartedly. "What do you need from me?"

Oren and I glanced at each other, and I nodded for him to answer. "I've taken Drake to all the places Alston and Sorcha had often gone to in the mortal realm together. We can't get a feel for her anywhere and I'm afraid we won't if what Drake suspects are true."

"What is it that you suspect?" she asked, looking at me.

I replied, "We think she might be somewhere that's muted her powers. She's not able to communicate with Oren so I'm only assuming the place she's in is surrounded by dark magic."

"And how can I help?"

"We need to know if you have any idea where he could've taken her other than the places we've already been." Oren went into detail on all the places we'd been while Sarette followed along, furrowing her brows in concentration.

Taking a deep breath, she turned her back on me and faced the window. "I think I might know where they're at," she whispered. "I don't know for sure, but it's worth a shot."

"Where?" I belted out quickly.

When Sarette faced us, fresh tears stained her cheeks. Her voice quivered when she asked, "What are you going to do if they're there? Are you going to kill Alston?"

Oren and I glanced at each other quickly. I wanted to kill Alston for what he'd done, and if he didn't hand Sorcha over then I *would* kill him. I wasn't sure what Sarette was expecting me to say, but she had to know that even though she was Sorcha's best friend, I couldn't let Alston live for her sake. That might be cruel, but it was the way it had to be. No one betrayed our people and lived.

"I'm sorry, Sarette, but it's entirely up to your cousin. If he hands Sorcha over willingly, I might consider not killing him, but if he doesn't then I will fight for her, and he *will* die."

She blew out a shaky breath. "Then I'm coming with you. I can talk to him ... get him to back down."

"No!" Oren and I yelled at the same time.

Narrowing her eyes, she pinned us with the most stubborn stare imaginable. It made me miss Sorcha even more, and it didn't help matters that Sarette had the same long, black hair and body that reminded me of her. "I'm afraid you have no choice. If you don't let me come then I'm not going to tell you where they might be. There's still a chance I'm wrong anyway. I only know of this place because I heard Alston talking about it, and I followed him. I figured it was his retreat when he would get upset over Sorcha."

"It's too dangerous, Sarette, and if we have to kill Alston you're going to be right there. Is that what you want? Do you really want to watch your cousin die?" I asked skeptically.

She gave me a defiant stare and pursed her lips. "No, I don't want to watch him die. That's why I'm hoping he'll give himself up when he sees me."

If Sarette was anything like Sorcha, she'd weasel her way into going no matter what I did or said. Huffing out a breath, I relented and gave in. "Fine! But if you want to be naïve enough to think Alston's going to listen to you then that's your problem. If things turn for the worse, you need to stay out of the way. Sorcha's probably going to be pissed as hell with me for bringing you, especially if you get hurt."

Sarette shrugged. "She'll just have to get over it. She helped rescue me and now I'm going to help rescue her. It'll make us even."

I couldn't argue with that. "Let's go," I told them. "I have a feeling this will be it."

Chapter Nineteen

I woke up extra early with an idea in my head. If I was surrounded by dark magic then there had to be an end point. There was no way it could cover that much land in the mortal realm, and not give out or have weak points. All I needed to do was sneak out of the house and see how far it took to get my connection to Oren open, and then hurry back once I talked to him.

Quietly stepping out of bed, I tiptoed to the closet. My warrior gear was in there along with my spear. The clanking sound of my armor made me cringe each time the sound vibrated across the room. Opening the door, I glanced around quickly before walking past what I assumed was the room Alston slept in. The door was closed, so I glided carefully away from it, holding my breath for emphasis.

The stairs creaked as I descended them and I silently cursed the whole time, hoping I wasn't screwing up my stealthy plan. If I could only get to the door I'd be able to get out. The front door opened silently and I was about to make a run for it when Alston's voice boomed out from behind me.

"Where the fuck do you think you're going?" he stormed angrily.

Not expecting his furious tone, I whirled around and faced him. He had never talked to me like that, and I definitely wasn't going to allow him to do it again. "First off!" I exclaimed. "Don't you ever use that tone with me again. Second, I'm not a prisoner, and if I want to go for a walk on my own then I'm entitled to. I don't need a babysitter, and you sure as hell are not going to order me around."

His electric blue eyes widened in panic, but only for a second. He approached me slowly as if I were a caged animal in need of a tranquilizer. I could recognize that maneuver from anywhere. He was preparing to chase me if I ran. My instincts told me to run, but with him inching closer I knew I wouldn't get far. My time for escape had already left.

When he was close enough, he lifted his hands up in defeat. "I'm sorry. I shouldn't have gotten overbearing like that. You just looked like you were trying to sneak off."

I was, I thought to myself, but I wasn't going to tell him that. So instead, I said, "I was trying to be quiet and not wake you."

"What were you going out there to do?" he asked, curious.

197

Nonchalantly, I shrugged my shoulders. "I wanted to get some fresh air and walk around a bit, maybe even practice with my spear. I still need to keep up with my training, you know."

He peered at me skeptically. "Are you sure you weren't trying to run away?"

"Now why would I do that? Do you have a guilty conscience or something?" I asked, studying his expression.

He laughed nervously and averted his eyes, a clear sign of lying. "No," he replied. "I just don't want you to leave without protection. I think you scared me more than anything."

I nodded, pretending to understand. "You know I'm not helpless, right? I have been training for a while and I have no doubt that I could kick your ass."

Alston bit his lip and moved gracefully to tower over me. "I think I'd like that. How about we do a little hand on hand combat outside for a while? Maybe it'll relieve some of the tension."

"You're on." I laughed wickedly. "Don't get mad when you get your ass beat."

He winked. "I'll take my chances."

My muscles ached, but I made sure to give Alston a good beating. "I think we're done with weapons for a while. By the way, where did you learn to do what you did with your spear? I know Oren and your brother didn't teach you those moves." He paused and furrowed his brows, looking off into the distance. "It actually kind of reminds me of how the Summer Fae fight."

After he said that his body tensed, but when he saw me watching him he relaxed, even though it looked forced. "Well, I don't know where I would've learned it from," I claimed. "Not unless someone from the Summer Court trained me."

Alston laughed nervously. "No, that couldn't be it. You don't ever spend time with anyone from the Summer other than Calista and Meliantha, and they aren't even Summer Fae anymore."

I didn't need magic to hear the bold faced lie in his statement. He still wouldn't even look me in the eye when he spoke either. *Now all I needed was to come up with a plan, but what?* I wondered. My momentary distraction cost me a swift kick to the leg from Alston, making me fall to the ground with a loud thump. The breath whooshed out of me when I made impact.

"Ow!" I groaned furiously.

Alston appeared above me, smiling. "You weren't paying attention, baby. Besides, it was funny watching you fall on your ass."

I scowled at him and quickly got to my feet. "You're going to pay for that," I hissed. All I needed was a few good hits on him to incapacitate him, and then I could make a run for it. By no means was I afraid of Alston, so if he did catch me I could defend myself, but I was hoping it wouldn't come to that. My main concern at the moment was contacting Oren.

Alston's wicked grin didn't help my growing anger as we circled each other. "You are so damn sexy when you're mad. It makes for good make-up sex."

I rolled my eyes. "I wouldn't count on it."

"Oh come on, Sorcha, you know you want it. You've always been an insatiable woman," he teased.

"Will you shut up?" He was goading me and I fell right into it. He loved to see me angry, and he got his wish. I dodged his attacks, except when the opportunity presented itself I went in for the hit. I landed a hard jab to Alston's jaw, making his head turn away from me with a snap. Not wasting any time, I made a run for it, and didn't look back.

"Sorcha!" Alston yelled. He chased after me, and with his long legs and my magic dampened I couldn't use my earth abilities to help slow him down. I didn't get too far before his weight barreled into me and he landed on top, crushing me to the ground. I struggled to breathe as his weight pinned me beneath him.

"What the hell was that?" he growled in my face.

I smirked. "It was a love tap," I said sarcastically.

"You deserved it for pissing me off."

He rubbed his jaw and shook his head. "I love to see you pissed, but not like that. It still turned me on though," he teased.

Huffing, I sighed, "Whatever, Alston. Do you mind getting off me?"

He pushed his body into me further, and I could definitely tell my anger turned him on from the hard bulge pressing up against my leg. His forearms closed me in as he leaned on his elbows, looking down at me. "I kind of like it here. You've never complained about me being on top before."

Alston lowered his head to kiss me, but I turned my head away before our lips could touch. "Well, I'm complaining now. I'm going to ask again, do you mind getting off of me?"

His growl was menacing, but he slowly lifted up his body and got to his feet. "What happened to you? We were hot and heavy back home, fucking anywhere and everywhere we could."

"Yeah, maybe ten months ago," I mumbled.

"Excuse me," he said quickly, alarmed.

I waved him off. "Nothing, just forget I said anything." His grip was bruising when he encircled my arms, pulling me up against him. "Alston, you're hurting me," I warned, gritting my teeth.

He didn't let me go, but held me there, studying my face. "You know something, don't you?"

"Like what?" I asked incredulously. "You're

acting as if you have something to hide. Maybe *you* know something I don't."

We stared each other down until something caught his eye over my shoulder. "Fuck!" he hissed. Grabbing my arm forcefully, he hurried me in the direction of the house.

"What's going on? What did you see?" I asked anxiously.

He kept dragging me behind him, and when I snuck a glance behind me I saw nothing. I tried to root my feet to the ground, but instead of me standing my ground it only infuriated Alston more. He picked me up and slung me over his shoulder, running the rest of the way to the house. When we got there, he kicked the door open and dropped me on the floor. Thankfully, I landed on my feet and not on my ass again.

Glaring at him, I crossed my arms over my chest. "I hope that's not the way you take your wife over the threshold when you get married," I quipped sarcastically.

"I just did," he sneered. "Welcome home, honey."

"You're serious, aren't you?"

His sneer grew into an all-out wicked grin. The mask had been lifted from his face, and what I saw was not the Alston I knew and cared about months ago. His eyes showed the cruelty and possessiveness that I'd always known was there, but hidden. He stalked toward me with long and determined strides, saying along the way, "You're mine, Sorcha, and no one is going to take you away from me."

I began taking steps back to get away from Alston's predatory gaze, but he kept advancing. "Why did you rush me in here? What's out there? Or better yet ... who's out there?"

"It doesn't matter who it is. You're not going anywhere."

"Like hell I'm not," I warned him. "Tell me, at what point did you decide to turn on our people?"

He stalked closer. "The moment I lost you."

"That doesn't flatter me, Alston. Did you think you wouldn't get caught?"

He furrowed his brows and opted to ignore my question with a wave of dismissal. "What I want to know is how you found out. Your memories are gone."

I laughed sarcastically. "I may not have my memories, but I'm not stupid. You may have the house concealed, and my magic blocked, but I can still feel that something's wrong with you."

"You know, I'm shocked they found you. No one knows of this place, and since they can't see it or sense us they'll pass right on by. I would love to be able to see Drake's face if he knew I fucked you while he was just yards away. You *will* be mine and mine only for the rest of your life. You might as well get used to it, even if I have to force you."

"Wait!" I held up my hand. "Are you saying he's actually out there right now?"

"Yes, it's him and your worthless guardian. Isn't it a shame you can't join them. Oh well, at least you'll be having fun with me in here."

"Not likely."

He was stalking me like a lion would before he pounced. The door was too far away, and my only chance to get there was going to be to fight my way there. I took off for the door only to be tackled to the floor by Alston's hulking frame. He pinned my arms above my head and immediately began leaving bruising kisses along my jaw down to my neck. His laugh sounded evil in my ear, making me cringe away from him. He held both of my wrists with one of his hands while the other began ripping away my armor. I struggled against his grasp as he lifted my shirt and ran his hand over my bare breast. He was so heavy on top of me I couldn't move, he was just too strong. He forcefully separated my legs with his knee and ground me into the floor by thrusting hard against me.

"It turns me on when you make it hard on me," he growled low in my ear.

"Is it going to turn you on when I kill you?" I hissed back angrily. "Because once I get out that door, you're dead."

He laughed. "I guess it's a good thing you're not getting to that door then, huh?"

"We'll see about that!"

With all my energy, I bucked my hips as hard as I could. Once his hand wavered, I freed one of my arms and slammed my elbow hard into the side of his face. He grunted with the impact and his body moved enough that I was able to knee him in the groin. He toppled over to the side and tried to make a grab for me, except I slipped out of his reach just in time to make a run for it. Scrambling across the floor, I made it to the door and pushed it open. Drake's eyes caught mine the moment I became visible, and relief flashed over his face.

I bolted straight for him, but the pain that radiated through my ribs stopped me. A snarling Alston was behind my back with one arm squeezing the breath out of my lungs, and the other holding a very sharp, iron knife at my throat.

Chapter Twenty

The moment she appeared, I wasted no time in running toward her, except I didn't get too far when I was stopped by an invisible force. It felt like a thick, unbreakable glass wall, sturdy and indestructible. Oren ran up beside me and punched it with all the force he could muster. The only sounds I heard were his audible cry of pain, and the bones that broke into tiny pieces in his hand.

Alston bellowed, "Having problems getting through?"

"You're done, Alston! Let her go!" I ordered, gritting my teeth.

Sorcha was angry, her chest heaving with furious breaths as she searched for an escape. Our eyes met briefly, and I hoped she understood the message I sent to her. Just off to her left, on the ground, was her spear. It was the only weapon there that could kill Alston, other than Oren's dagger he had strapped on his belt. However, that was a lost cause since Oren and I couldn't go past the barrier.

Panic showed behind the surface of Alston's gaze, but he was trying to hide it. I could usually handle tense situations, but this one was more difficult considering Alston was unstable with a knife to Sorcha's throat, and it wasn't just an ordinary knife either.

"Do you see what I see?" I pointed out to Oren.

He shifted angrily on his feet. "Unfortunately, yes. The knife is made of iron."

Alston planned it well. He held the iron knife in a gloved hand. If he wasn't wearing that glove, the iron would've eaten through his skin in a matter of seconds. "She's not going anywhere," he said, squeezing Sorcha tighter against him. The knife grazed her skin when he moved, causing it to sizzle and burn on contact.

She hissed in pain. "You're going to pay for that!"

"Not if you're dead," he replied darkly.

My anger boiled over the edge, the dragon stirring underneath my skin, ready to kill. No one threatens what's mine, except I knew Alston's admission was not a threat. He would kill her to keep her from me. I could see in his eyes how obsessed he was with her.

Backing up from the invisible shield, I spread my arms open in invitation. "You don't want to kill her, you fool. This is about me. It's always been about me, and your jealousy over the fact that the one woman you want is destined to be with me. You're a coward hiding behind the dark sorcerer's evil, and what's worse is that you feel like a man apprehending her when she's at her weakest. You'd be shitting yourself right now if she had her powers."

He snarled. "I would rather see her dead than in your arms. If that means I have to hide behind walls to have her, then I will. She's mine!" The knife touched her skin again, making her grimace in pain. Only one slight jab and that iron would flow through her veins and kill her. I had to do something.

"Why don't we fight for her then?" I asked, ready and determined to end it quickly. "Whoever wins gets her. Unless you're too much of a chicken shit to fight me."

"Are you kidding me?!" Sorcha shouted in disbelief.

Alston ignored her and narrowed his eyes at me, contemplating my offer. "How do I know Oren won't try to steal Sorcha away if I win? How do I know you'll keep up the bargain?"

"You have my promise, you worthless traitor."

Alston chuckled, and thankfully dropped the knife from the Sorcha's throat, although he still held her in a vice-like grip against his chest. "You really are an arrogant dick, you know that. I need you to also promise that no one will come searching for me and Sorcha after all of this is over."

Oren grabbed my arm, and hissed in my ear, "Are you crazy? Either you *are* very arrogant and stupid, or you're extremely confident. If you fail, we lose her. Think carefully, Your Highness, because if you lose I will *not* let him take her. You condemn us both to death with your promise."

Promises were sacred with our people, and once you made one you had to uphold it. If you didn't there would be consequences, mostly resulting in death. Keeping my eyes on Alston and Sorcha, I leaned over to Oren and whispered, "Trust me."

Oren scoffed in outrage, and forced himself to back away. Sarette was nowhere to be seen, and we had planned it that way. We didn't want her appearing until the time was right. Impatiently, I announced, "Do you accept the challenge, or are you going to hide? What better way is there to prove how much you want her by fighting me? We both know her very well, Alston. She doesn't like weak men. You'll never get her love if you cower behind your fear."

Sorcha's lethal gaze could've killed me where I stood, and in that moment I was glad she didn't have her powers. She obviously didn't approve of my methods, but I had to do something to get that knife away from her throat.

Alston glared at me for a few hard minutes, and then finally relented. "I accept," he answered, slowly releasing Sorcha from his grip.

Although, what happened next was definitely a Sorcha move and one I should've expected. She punched Alston square in the nose, causing blood to spray out and splatter across the ground. "I don't accept!" she snapped angrily, glaring at both me and her blood-drenched captor. "How dare you both negotiate my freedom in front of me? I can fight my own battles with or without my magic. Never have I *ever* needed a man to fight for me, and it sure as hell isn't going to start today." Directing her venom to Alston, she said, "If you want me, you're going to have to fight *me*, not Drake."

"No!" I ordered forcefully.

"And ..." she began, holding up a hand to cut me off. "If I lose, I will willingly stay in the mortal realm with Alston."

Alston gleamed at the new proposition, and immediately set his hungry eyes on her. "Sorry, Prince Drake, but I believe the princess has offered me a better deal."

I hit the wall in protest. "Dammit, Sorcha! For once why can't you swallow your pride?"

She tore her eyes away from Alston and smirked at me. "If you know me as well as you say you do then you should be used to it by now."

"Sorcha!" Oren demanded. "Don't do this!"

Sorcha's face softened with a hint of a smile. She didn't say anything, but mouthed the words 'trust me' to him. Oren threw his hands up in the air and punched the wall again. "You both are going to drive me crazy! What the hell is she going to do?"

Shaking my head, I replied, "I don't know, but I'm dying to find out. She's always been one of surprises."

Sorcha picked up her spear and advanced on Alston. "Let's get this done," she spat at him.

"With pleasure, baby." Alston licked his lips and advanced, looking like a wolf searching for its prey. Hearing him speak to her in that voice made my blood boil and the dragon inside me tense. The thought of him touching her made me want to kill him. How I was going to be able to watch the fight, I didn't know. Alston deserved a slow and painful death.

Sorcha looked fierce and focused as she circled Alston. Her concentration was perfect when we would train together, and I knew in that moment that nothing could break her. Clenching my fists, I knew the attack was about to start, and I dreaded it. Alston struck out first and dove for Sorcha's legs, determined to get her to the ground. If he pinned her with his weight it'd be all over for her. His size was his only advantage whereas Sorcha was agile and light on her feet, and deadly with her spear.

Sorcha landed some good blows to his face, but Alston kept going strong. The prize was right in front of him, and he wasn't going to stop until he had her. He was relentless, and I was helpless having to watch.

All Sorcha needed to do was stab him with her spear and it would end him; however, things took a turn for the worse when Alston threw Sorcha to the ground and grabbed her spear. Sorcha landed hard on her knees and turned around in time to watch Alston snap her spear in half, and throw the pieces to the ground as if it were trash. His evil laugh penetrated the air, knowing he hit her with a low blow.

She flinched when she heard the audible crack of her spear splitting in two, and immediately afterwards she let out the loudest war cry I'd ever heard. Her spear was sacred to her, and Alston just destroyed it. Breathing hard, I knew she was livid when all I saw on her face was vengeance. "This isn't good," Oren claimed. "She's pissed and we both know how impulsive she can get when she's like that."

"Yes, I know," I agreed. "I've seen her make mistakes when I was training with her in our dreams. She lets her emotions get the best of her sometimes, especially when she's really angry."

Sorcha's rage consumed her, and that rage blinded her. Alston got the upper hand, and took her to the ground, straddling her waist. Her legs were pinned beneath his body while Alston's arms held hers to the side. Alston winked at me, and I scowled at him before he looked down at Sorcha. "Do you give in?" he asked her.

When she didn't answer he slammed her head into the ground. She winced and screamed in pain.

With her jaw clenched, she lifted her chin defiantly. He repeated, "Do you give in?"

Expecting victory, a smile splayed on his face, but disappeared when Sorcha calmly said, "No."

Alston seethed with fury and slammed his forearm into her neck, cutting off her air. My fists were bloody from the incessant pounding on the invisible wall, but I kept hitting in hopes it would come down. Eventually, the wall began to waver and thin where I hit it with my bloodied hands. The places where my blood touched, it thinned. My eyes grew wide in delight and I smiled.

"Why the hell are you smiling?" Oren demanded. "There's nothing to smile about right now!"

Unsheathing my sword, I sliced the tip over my palm. The blood gushed out and I placed that bloody hand to the wall. Slowly, my hand started moving forward through the invisible barrier inch by inch. I could feel it giving away until there was nothing but air.

"How is this possible?" Oren whispered so Alston couldn't hear him.

"I'm not sure."

Sorcha was still refusing to give in, and soon I'd be in there rescuing her. When the wall fully opened, Sarette made her appearance and barreled past me, heading straight for Alston. His eyes grew wide and he faltered when he saw Sarette approaching him.

"How could you do this?" Sarette cried. "How

could you betray your people?"

Alston kept the pressure on Sorcha's neck, keeping her in place, but I could hear her wheezing for air. "I had to get what I want," he answered, looking wistfully down at Sorcha. "But now it's all over. I can't let him have her." Slowly, he leaned over and kissed Sorcha on the lips. "I'm so sorry, baby, but we'll meet each other again in the Hereafter."

Everything after that went into slow motion. With my sword drawn, I lunged the second I saw him pull out the iron dagger from his belt and aim it toward Sorcha's heart. Before the knife hit its mark, Sorcha unlocked one of her arms from Alston's grasp and knocked him onto his back. It took a few seconds to understand what happened, but then I saw the jagged stick protruding out of Alston's chest. Sorcha had stabbed him with her broken spear.

Sarette rushed to Alston's side, crying and wailing while I went to Sorcha's. I scooped her up in my arms and crushed her to me. "Are you okay?" I asked, holding her tight.

Sorcha rubbed her neck and grimaced. "Yeah, I'm fine. My neck hurts, but at least I can breathe again." I set her down so she could join her grieving friend while Alston choked out his dying words. Her face showed no remorse as he lay there dying on the ground. "All I wanted was to be with you," he stuttered weakly. "I loved you, Sorcha."

Sorcha regretfully shook her head and knelt

down on the ground beside him. "No, you didn't. If you truly loved me you wouldn't have done what you did. Good-bye, Alston." She backed away quickly when he tried to reach for her, and came to stand between me and Oren. Sorcha turned her back and slowly walked away.

When she was far enough away from Alston and Sarette, Sorcha flung herself into Oren's arms. "You had me worried, *ai dulin*," he whispered gruffly to her.

She sighed. "I told you to trust me, didn't I?"

He released her and lifted an eyebrow. "Sometimes that's hard to do with you."

They both laughed lightly. Sorcha came to my side and took my hand, holding it tight. "I knew what you were doing, by the way," she admitted. "Because I did the same thing."

"About what?" I asked, confused.

She looked up at me and grinned. "About the promise to hand me over if you lost the fight."

"Yeah, about that," Oren interrupted, glaring at me. "I was going to kill you myself if you let Alston have her."

Sorcha patted her guardian on the arm. "You had nothing to worry about, hence me telling you to trust me. The thing is, our promises don't hold power in the mortal realm. I could've promised him I'd stay with him forever and wouldn't have had to live by it. It was going to be my way of escape without putting anyone's lives in danger."

"I didn't know that promises didn't work here," Oren said sounding surprised. "Who told you that?"

Sorcha narrowed her eyes. "I'm not sure who told me, but I knew it was true somehow."

"I was the one who told you," I revealed confidently. "One time in our dreams we were discussing secrets that not many fae know, and that's when I told you that promises don't work in the mortal realm. I'd say that information came in handy today." I brought mine and Sorcha's clasped hand to my lips and kissed her knuckles while she watched me intently. "There was no way I'd ever promise to let someone else have you."

"Deep down, I knew that, but it still made me mad to hear it," Sorcha added. "When do you think my memories will come back, or if I'll *ever* get them back?"

She looked back and forth between me and Oren. Her guardian shrugged, not knowing what to say, however I had an idea. "I think I know how," I revealed to her. "When we go back to the Land of the Fae there's somewhere I want to take you."

Her bright green eyes searched mine excitedly. "Where?" she asked.

"You'll see."

By the time everything was said and done, Sarette finally joined us, holding the tip of Sorcha's spear in her hand, and handed it to Sorcha. "This was on the ground after Alston turned to ash. I thought you might want it back."

Sorcha flinched when she took it, not upset over killing Alston, but upset for causing her friend pain. She folded Sarette into her arms and held her close while her friend cried for her loss. "I'm so sorry, Sarette. I didn't want it to end the way it did, but there was no other choice."

"I know," Sarette whispered.

Reluctantly, Sorcha pulled away and glanced behind her to the pile of ash on the ground, the pile of ash that used to be her lover, friend, and traitor. When she spotted me staring at her, she gave me a small smile. "I'm ready to go home. I'm ready to remember."

No one said a word as Oren made the portal to lead us back home. If my idea worked, Sorcha would have her memories back, and be at her home where she belonged … with me.

"Are you sure this will work?" Oren asked.

"I'm not sure, but it's worth a try. Send word to all the courts about what happened. I'll bring Sorcha back soon." Oren bowed his head and said his good-bye to Sorcha. I began taking off my clothes and tossing them to the ground once Oren and Sarette were out of sight. I was going to fly Sorcha to the place we needed to go, to the place I could feel calling to us once we stepped back into the Land of the Fae.

"Do you need me to hold your clothes?" Sorcha asked. Her tone was humor-filled while her eyes were alight with fire. Even though she didn't remember our time together, I could still feel a want inside of her. It was a good sign.

"Yes, please. Unless you want me to walk around naked when we get to where I'm taking you."

She shook her head and chuckled, gathering my clothes. "Do whatever you want. I'm not complaining."

After she had my clothes piled in her arms, I started the transformation. She stood in awe as my dragon side appeared before her. "Wow," she breathed once it was all over.

I lowered my body to the ground so she could climb up. When I felt her settled and holding on tight, I lifted off into the sky. I could see for miles and miles away when I was in the air. The Summer Court was green and lush with life as we flew across the expanse of it. The place I was taking her was so close I could feel the pull tugging on my insides and guiding my wings there. When our destination appeared, I landed smoothly on the ground and waited for Sorcha to slide off my back before I transformed into my body.

She handed me my clothes and walked away from me as if she were in a daze. "I can sense it calling to me," she whispered, hooking a glance over her shoulder at me.

"So can I."

She glided slowly across the ground, but then stopped and knelt down, placing her hands on the dry earth below her. The land vibrated with energy, and immediately burst forth with new life the moment her hands made contact. It was surreal how it all happened so suddenly. The sea we had dreamed of now filled up the horizon as far as we could see, and below our feet was the soft, white sand. Sorcha giggled as the water flowed over her hands and legs, soaking her with its warm embrace. When she turned around, tears flooded her eyes … happy tears, and she was beaming.

"I remember," she murmured softly. "I remember everything."

Chapter Twenty-One

Sorcha

The look of relief on Drake's face was heartwarming. I knew he was worried about it not working by bringing me to our land, but it did. He scooped me into his arms and kissed me with more passion than I ever thought imaginable. His tongue devoured mine with such intensity that I could feel the longing come off of him in waves.

Not wanting to separate from his kisses, reluctantly I did. "I'm so sorry, Drake. I never imagined I'd ever lose my memories of you. I don't know what I would've done if I spent the rest of my life not remembering what we had."

Drake shook his head and placed both his hands on my face. "You would've remembered in time. You found me in your dreams even though you lost your memories. That right there says that no matter what happens to us we will always remember each other ... one way or another."

"How did you find me?" I asked curiously. "I

never heard you or Oren say."

"Sarette was the one who found you. She overheard Alston saying something about a house he had in the mortal realm. She followed him and saw for herself. Oren and I searched all the places you and Alston used to frequent together, but of course, they were all the wrong ones."

I knew Drake wanted to ask me something, but was a little hesitant to ask. His jaw muscle clenched over and over, and I'd recognized that from before as being a nervous tick he got. The infamous dragon had a nervous streak that only I had ever seen.

Rubbing his jaw with my hand, I gazed into his smoky gray eyes and asked, "What's wrong, Drake? Just ask me what you have on your mind. I know something's troubling you."

Not taking his eyes off mine, he finally revealed his distress. "I kept telling myself it wouldn't matter, and it doesn't now that Alston's dead, but did he take advantage of you when you were with him? Did you two sleep together?"

"No!" I shrieked loudly. "We slept in the same bed one night, but never did anything more than that. Even though I didn't remember you, I still didn't want him like that. My heart was claimed before he took my memories."

It never occurred to me that those thoughts would be eating away at his mind. I would've been livid if he was alone with a past lover with no recollection of who I was. Drake smiled wryly. "I thought you said you never wanted to be claimed. Does this mean you're mine?"

"Yes, you knew that already."

"Always?"

"Yes."

"How can I get you to prove it?" he asked smoothly.

Lifting my hands, I ran them through his silky red strands. His gray eyes were filled with humor, waiting on a snarky comeback from me. For the first time, he wasn't going to get one. I kissed him gently on the lips and took in a deep, calming breath of his Summer scent.

"I love you, Drake. I spent my whole life living in my mother's shadow until you came along. You brought me a love so scorching yet tender that I was bound to be melted by it. I give you my heart freely. Take it, claim it, and hold it as your own. I will always and forever be yours, my love. *Amin mela lle ilyamemie ar' ten' oio.*"

After saying the words in the Old Fae language, I felt a sense of peace flow through my veins. I could feel my inner frost slowly melting inch by inch. Drake was speechless, frozen in place and stunned into silence. I knew he wasn't expecting me to make the eternal bond at that moment, and it felt good catching him off guard.

"All of this time," he began, "I've never heard

you say anything like that, but I'm glad you did."

I grinned. "I know, and I've regretted not saying anything like that before. I may not express my feelings a whole lot in words, but I do love you. I would just rather show you with actions instead of words."

"I understand," he whispered against my lips. "I may not be a man that can share my feelings too well with words either, but I will spend the rest of my life trying. I love you, Sorcha. You broke my hard exterior, opening my eyes and my heart. As I've claimed your heart and soul, you've claimed mine. I promise to keep yours safe for the rest of our lives, always and forever. *Amin mela lle ilyamemie ar' ten' oio.* Our bond is now sealed."

He kissed me gently to seal the bond of our words, but we still needed to do one more thing to completely fulfill the marriage bond and complete our land. Drake broke away from the kiss, both of us breathless. "Damn, I want make love to you so bad, and not just in our dreams. I want to feel the real you beneath me."

I licked my eager lips. "Then take me."

His hungered words had me panting with need. I'd felt his lips on my body plenty of times in my dreams, but I knew it would be better once it was real. "Are you sure it's not too soon. You've been through so much the past couple of days. I don't want to rush you."

Exasperated, I shook my head. "You're not rushing me. If anything, I'm rushing you. We need this, I need this. Besides, we've already made love in our dreams. I know what I'm getting into."

Drake smirked, and held me tighter against him while grazing his lips along my neck. "That was nothing compared to what it'll be like now. I need you too much to go slow."

I smiled. "I think you read my mind, but where?"

Drake's grin was intoxicating. He nodded his head in the direction of the water and said, "I think right there in the water. Take a look."

When I turned my head and saw what he was looking at, I gasped in wonder. "What did you do?"

Drake came up beside me and shrugged. "Well, I was thinking about how I could just take you out here in the open, not caring who came by or who saw us. However, I didn't think that would work with you, so I asked the land to help."

"And what exactly did you ask it?"

"I was thinking in my head how I wanted everything to be special, and how we needed a hidden place that was comfortable yet romantic. I guess the water is doing our bidding like it did in our dreams."

My mind was in awe at the sight before me. The water had pulled back, making a path down the center. It led down into an opening, but I couldn't see the bottom. I had no clue what awaited us in the watery depths. "This is strange," I thought out loud.

Drake grabbed my hand and pulled me to the water. "Yes, it is, but at least we get to experience it together. It's but one of our many adventures. Now we can do it for real instead of in our dreams."

"Are you implying that you want to forego our dream realm adventures?" I asked.

He laughed. "Definitely not. I just don't want anyone else in your dreams other than me."

We walked down the path while walls of water closed in beside us. I grazed my hand across the surface and felt the energy soaking into my skin. We kept going further, deeper and deeper, and when I looked back, the water was closing off the path behind us. It was exciting yet terrifying to know we were surrounded by water that could close in on us at any moment, but I knew that it wouldn't happen. It was our sea, our court … mine and Drake's.

The end of the path opened up, and Drake and I both froze at the sight before us. The water had enclosed all around us, giving us the privacy from the outside world. Letting go of Drake's hand, I walked around the underwater room. "This is amazing," I breathed.

The bed frame was made of white corral and pearls. The blankets on top shimmered with the reflection of the sun through the watery ceiling. I touched the top of the bed and my hand almost sank into its softness. The smells were so exotic and fresh that I couldn't stop breathing it and soaking it into my skin. It was incredible, and so full of life.

Drake came up behind me and wrapped his arms around my waist. "Will this do?" he asked huskily. He pressed his body firmly against my back and began kissing along my neck. It sent chills through my body and I shivered. "Don't worry, beautiful. I'll keep you warm."

Releasing a shaky breath, I sighed. "I already am."

I wasn't exactly dressed for seduction, but it didn't seem to bother Drake as he removed the bits and pieces of my warrior gear off my body, throwing it all to the floor. I climbed backwards onto the bed while he prowled over the top of me, spearing me with his heated gaze. Slowly, he lifted my shirt, leaving wet kisses up my stomach and over my breasts before he slipped it over my head. I groaned as he bit my nipple playfully before moving down to take off my pants.

Drake watched me like a ravenous animal. His heat-filled gaze never left mine the whole time he slid the pants down my legs. Propping myself on my elbows, I bit my lip and watched in fascination as he slowly removed his clothes, teasing me. The bulge in his pants was straining to be let out, and for the life of me I couldn't tear my gaze away.

When Drake finally lowered his pants, I groaned. I was wet and ready for the taking. He kissed his way up my leg, starting with my ankle, up to my knees, and along my inner thighs where he nipped my tender spots. Once he reached my stomach, he trailed his tongue all the way up until he reached my breasts while testing my readiness with his fingers. He groaned once he realized how wet I was for him. Licking and sucking on my sensitive nipple, he thrust his fingers inside me while rubbing my swollen nub with the pad of his thumb. The sensation of both had me immediately coming and shouting out my release.

I arched off the bed and gasped, "You're killing me, Drake."

He shook his head. "No beautiful, you're killing me. I almost lost it feeling you clench around my fingers. I like knowing my touch brings you pleasure."

"It brings more than pleasure," I revealed, throwing him on his back on the bed, straddling him. "It drives me crazy."

I was the one starved and hungry as I savagely descended upon his lips, tasting and biting. While rubbing my sensitive breasts along his chest, I moved my core over his straining cock, teasing him.

Drake gripped my hips and growled, "I want to be inside you, now." His tone implied he was about to lose control, and as much as I wanted to torment him I couldn't. I needed him too much.

I lifted my hips slowly, only letting the tip of his erection graze my opening, before I gently lowered myself onto his pulsating cock. "Is that better?" I whispered hoarsely.

He held my hips, rocking me gently back and forth, going slowly until my body accommodated to his size. He filled me completely, stretching me, but I needed more. Digging my nails into his shoulders, I slammed down on him as hard as I could. Drake bucked underneath me and took in a sharp breath. "I'm not going to last long with you doing that."

"You said it yourself earlier. Your need is too great to go slow ... well, so is mine."

To stop him from speaking, I captured his lips and imprisoned his tongue with my own. My body rocked hard against him, and I could feel his cock straining with the first taste of orgasm. I rode him until the tingling in my core exploded all around me, clenching tight around his shaft until he couldn't hold out any longer. He gripped my hips harder and bit into my shoulder as he came. The pain from his bite was arousing and made the aftermath of my orgasm that much sweeter as tiny tremors racked my body. Slowly, I stopped my hips from moving and collapsed on top of him, satiated and breathing hard.

The mist of water from the wall around us sprinkled us with cold dew. It sizzled across my heated skin, which was now the color and warmth of Drake's, not the pale and cold skin of the Winter Fae. When I focused on the swirling mist, I realized it wasn't water sprinkling us, but magic, the magic of our land. Still connected, I sat up slowly and watched the blue swirling magic of my court flow through the room.

Each court was different with its changes. Calista and Ryder got their crowns, Meliantha and Kalen got their glittery skin and tattoos, but I wondered was going to happen to me and Drake. Drake was already a Summer Fae, so I knew whatever was going to happen was going to happen to me. My body looked normal, except for my golden skin that used to be pale. Although, when I glanced down at Drake, I knew it wasn't so.

Drake grabbed my face with both hands and pulled me down to him, searching frantically over my face. He was amazed, shocked, and utterly surprised. "What is it, Drake? What do you see?" He opened his mouth and closed it, and then did it again. "What is it?" I asked again.

"It's amazing," he breathed, staring at me in awe.

I searched around the room for a mirror, and of course there wasn't one. I had to know what would cause him to look at me like that. Only when I saw my reflection in the wall of water did I understand. Sitting up slowly, I slid off of Drake's body and walked toward the girl staring back at me in the water. What I saw in the reflection was nothing like I expected. My mouth was wide open in shock, but my eyes … my eyes were no longer the same. As crazy as it sounded, I touched my face to make sure it was real, and blinked to see if my eyes would change back. They didn't.

"What does this mean?" I asked quietly, talking to myself.

Drake came up behind me and kissed my cheek. "It means, my Queen, that I'm no longer alone or one of a kind in our land. With this change you'll be as fierce as me and definitely one to be feared. Your cunning mind along with this gift will make you a scary thing to behold." He smiled at me in the reflection. "The Summer Court has just gained another queen, and another ... dragon."

My breath hitched at hearing him say it out loud. In that moment, Drake's eyes mirrored mine. His gray eyes with the slit-like pupils stared back at me just like my green ones stared back at him in the reflection. My eyes were brighter, more dangerous, hiding the massive beast that lurked beneath.

"I wonder what I'm going to look like, if I'll be the same color as you or a different type of dragon altogether. How do I go through the change?"

"I'll show you how to do everything, don't worry, and I'm sure you're going to be a beautiful dragon. I never imagined I'd have another dragon to fly with after being alone for so long." He padded over to the bed and took a seat, watching me in wonder.

"How do you get your eyes to change back?" I asked curiously.

Drake shrugged and smiled mischievously at me.

"When your emotions are heightened it brings the dragon closer to the front. In this case, we were both sexually aroused and it looks like you still are. That might be why they haven't changed."

I smirked, and raked my gaze over his still hard body. "I could say the same for you, you know."

"You're right." He nodded, beckoning me toward the bed with a crook of his finger. "It's my time to make love to you."

The blue mist swirled around the room, bringing a whole new surge of energy, fueling me with desire. I glided back to the bed, ready to be devoured by my king, lover, and husband. Once I got into reaching distance, Drake grabbed my wrist and pulled me to the bed. Lowering me onto my back, he settled himself beside me.

Whispering softly, he asked, "You're not upset, are you? About the change I mean. It's definitely something to get used to."

"I'm happy about the change," I assured him. "It brings me a lot closer to you because now I'll understand and be able to share this part of your life with you."

"I'm glad to hear it. Now let's see if we can get those dragon eyes to disappear for a while." He winked at me and climbed over my body, separating my legs with his knee. "I love you," he whispered as he lowered his lips to mine, kissing me softly.

His hard cock pressed against my opening, ready

to take me with one hard thrust. Slowly, I wrapped my legs around his waist and whispered back, "I love you, too."

Drake kept his eyes on me the whole time he entered me, inch by inch, deeper and deeper until he was fully inside. His eyes flickered from dragon to normal with each thrust and I knew mine were doing the same. He pleasured me and teased me for the rest of the evening, until we were both exhausted from the stressful events of the past two days plus the many hours of our love making. Running my fingers through his hair, I watched him as he fell asleep. He looked so peaceful, and I knew he'd be waiting for me in the dream realm, ready for more.

Once my eyes closed, I immediately entered into the dream realm.

"Good evening, Princess," the evil voice crooned lazily.

"What the …" I was expecting to see Drake, and was shocked to see Alasdair standing right behind me. Narrowing my eyes, I scowled at him in disgust. "If you must know, I'm a Summer queen now. Surely,

one of your spies has told you by now."

"Yes, I found out. Congratulations, by the way. I knew your idiot of an old lover wouldn't be able to hold onto you for long."

With my arms across my chest, I glowered at him with all the hate in my body I could muster. "Why are you here in my dreams? I'm sure you can find other people to mess with that actually give a damn."

He smiled. "Oh, this is only going to be a one-time thing, although, I do find your witty banter humorous. I thought I would gloat a bit and tell you what I'm up to."

Impatient, I threw my hands up in the air. "I don't care what you're up to. You're the one who must have something to prove since you want to throw it in my face. Are you trying to compensate for something lacking, sorcerer? Frankly, it's pretty pathetic."

His smile instantly left and was replaced with rage. The next second he had my throat in his crushing grip, and pulled me to him. "My, my ... you sure do have a sharp tongue for one who's about to lose everything once I win this battle. See, this is the reason why I didn't want another Winter bitch to fuck around with. You talk too fucking much."

"Thank the heavens for that," I rasped.

He snarled at me and let go. "I'm done wasting my time with you. Now that I have the scroll, only I know where it's located. So this time you won't have a pathetic weakling who can tell you where it's at."

"We'll figure out something," I said, determined.

He bellowed, shaking his head. "Keep dreaming, Your Highness. While you all scramble around like idiots, I'm building a nice mortal army to destroy you. Just imagine what it would be like to have all those iron weapons here wreaking havoc on your weak faerie blood."

Gritting my teeth, I kept my mouth shut for fear of giving something away. I had a secret of my own, but there was no way I was going to gloat about it.

"What, no comeback?" he teased. "I must've hit a weak spot for the mighty Sorcha not to have a retort. Very well then. On this note, I will leave you to your pathetic existence. Sweet dreams."

He disappeared quickly, leaving his evil stench behind as I stood alone in the vacant expanse of my dream. For now, I would let him think he had the upper hand, but really he was the one who was going to be made a fool of.

The sound of Drake's voice called me out of the dream world. "We have a busy day, beautiful. It's time to wake up." Groaning, I placed my hands over my eyes and rolled over. "Rough night?" he asked sarcastically.

"Wonderful night ... terrible dream."

Drake got off the bed and snatched his pants off the floor. "Yeah, it was terrible because I wasn't in it. I thought you would come to me last night." His gaze was playful, but I could sense he was curious as to why I didn't show up in his dream.

I sighed. "Trust me, I had no choice in my dream." Slowly, I swung my legs over the side of the bed and took a deep breath. Drake wasn't going to be happy when I told him the reason I didn't visit him was because of the dark sorcerer. He was still putting on his clothes when I peered over my shoulder. "The dark sorcerer came to me last night, Drake."

Drake froze and narrowed his eyes, all playfulness set aside. "You're serious, aren't you?"

I nodded. "Yes, and I know it was a real dream and not something I imagined. Now that he has my power, I guess he can dream walk, too. Although, he did say it was only going to be a one-time thing. I guess I can't really complain about that."

Frustrated, Drake ran his hands through his mussed up hair and came to kneel in front of me. He wrapped his arms around my waist and settled between my thighs. "He didn't hurt you, did he? What did he say?"

I kissed him on the lips. "Oh, just the usual. I

have your power, I'm going to take over the world, and you're all going to suffer … et cetera. Just the same old stuff he says every time he threatens one of us. He really wanted to gloat about the scroll, and how he's hidden it again where no one other than him knows where it's at. What really has me nervous is the fact he has mortals lined up to fight for him."

Drake's eyes grew wide and furious. "What the fuck? We have to stop him before that happens."

"I agree. We need to tell everyone, but to be on the safe side we need it to be only our families, no one else. We don't know who's with us and who isn't."

Drake nodded and rose to his feet. "Once you're dressed we'll go to shore and head to the palace. We'll figure out what to do and go from there once we talk to everyone. Then, I want to come back here and start our life together."

I grinned. "Me too."

Once I was dressed, the water began to open the path for us like it did when we came in. Drake took my hand, and we started up the sandy walkway. When it fully opened up to shore, we saw that we had some visitors waiting for us. Calista and Ryder were both grinning from ear to ear at our approach. My brother looked dashing in his all black attire being the smoldering bad boy of my family. Calista, on the other hand, looked ethereal with her wavy, blonde hair and emerald green riding dress that matched both mine and her eyes.

"Sorcha, you look amazing!" Calista exclaimed when I got closer.

Once Drake and I were on shore, she rushed over and hugged me and then moved to her brother. Ryder kissed me on the cheek—taking hold of my hands— and pulled them out from my sides. "Well, I guess it all makes sense now why you tried going to the tanning bed a few years ago. You must've always been meant to be a Summer Fae."

I chuckled. "I believe you're right, dear brother. Except now no tanning beds are necessary."

Drake pulled me into his side and placed his arm around my shoulder. He looked at Calista and Ryder, and asked, "What are you two doing here? We were actually getting ready to head back to the Summer Palace."

"No need for that," Calista explained. "Everyone is coming here. When Oren showed up and explained what happened, Father had us all summoned. Once I felt the land shift, I knew things had changed here. I couldn't wait any longer to see it for myself." She paused and glanced around in awe at what was now a tropical paradise. Exotic trees lined the white sandy shoreline, and the water … it was bluer than any body of water I'd ever seen. "I never thought in my life that this would happen. We have two Summer Courts now, or at least an extension of it. Your land is absolutely breathtaking."

"Thank you," Drake and I said simultaneously, smiling.

"How is Brayden?" I asked Ryder. "I knew he was injured in the battle and taken back to the Spring Court. I never had the chance to see if he was okay." Ryder shrugged and glanced over at Calista with a strange look on his face.

Calista snorted and burst out laughing. "Your brother is doing perfectly fine. I think he got a little more than he bargained for, though. Except, I don't think he's handling it as well as all of us had."

Confused, I eyed them both and asked, "What do you mean by that?"

Ryder sighed. "It appears our brother just had his vision with the lovely Ariella."

"What?" I shouted, excited. "This is definitely a momentous occasion. How did it happen?"

Calista grinned and answered, "It happened when she and Brayden were saying good-bye at the Spring Court. They made contact and had their vision right there in front of everyone. I heard Brayden turned all shades of red after that, and quickly walked away. I'd say this turn of events is very interesting."

Drake bellowed. "Oh, I can imagine. Ariella is a handful. I hope Brayden knows what he's getting into. Although, I'm pretty sure she was pissed if he just walked away from her."

Calista grabbed my hand and led me over to the water's edge. "I'm sure they'll do just fine with each other. Brayden wouldn't be her match if they couldn't." She paused and furrowed her brows, raking her gaze back and forth, clearly concentrating on something. "Okay, enough about visions. I think it's time we built up your palace. After all, everyone's coming to see you. With my magic and your brains we could come up with something spectacular. What do you say?"

Calista's grip on my hand was tight and reassuring, and her magic was so strong I could feel it pulsing throughout my body. She glanced at our clasped hands. "It's crazy, isn't it? When our powers combine like this it's the most amazing feeling I've ever felt. Just think of what I, you, Mel, and Ariella could do if we all combined our power."

"We would be invincible," I breathed.

Drake took that time to grab my other hand while Ryder took Calista's other. "Are we ready?" Calista asked, raising her eyebrows at me and Drake. "All you have to do is concentrate on what you want, and it'll happen."

I smiled at them all before closing my eyes. "Let's do this!"

Chapter Twenty-Two

Drake and Ryder welcomed our families while Calista helped me change clothes and get ready. "I'm sorry that Alston betrayed you. I know it had to be hard with losing your memories and all," Calista murmured gently while buttoning up my dress. The one shoulder masterpiece was sea blue ... Drake's favorite color on me.

"It *was* really hard. I hate to think about what would've happened if I didn't get my memories back."

"Thankfully, you don't have to worry about that." When she finished buttoning my dress, she turned me around to face her. "You know, when Ryder and I had our vision Drake swore that he'd never be in a situation like that. He thought our love was ridiculous and sappy. I probably need to give him hell like he did me and Meliantha, don't I?"

"Definitely!" I agreed.

We both began laughing. Suddenly, I felt the

connection in my mind open up, signaling that I wasn't alone. *"Everyone's waiting, ai dulin,"* Oren called out silently.

"Calista and I are almost done here. We just need a couple more minutes. How are my parents?"

Calista watched me with a sad, knowing smile lingering on her face. She turned her head away and walked over to the window, keeping her back to me.

"They're anxious to see you, but so is everyone else. Drake just told everyone about you being a dragon now."

In my head, I laughed. *"I knew he couldn't wait to tell everyone about that."*

"I guess it'll be you protecting me from now on. My, my, how the tables have turned. I don't think I've ever had to protect you."

"That's not true," I argued. *"You've always been there for me, and anyway, what's wrong with protecting each other? I can't help that you've been sworn to protect a girl who has the brains to get her out of sticky situations on her own. You don't always have to be the protector, you know."*

"Yes I do, ai dulin," he insisted. *"Now get yourself down here before your mother comes looking for you."*

"Will do." When I knew he was done talking, I focused my attention back on Calista. Her back was still to me, but her shoulders were hunched over and quaking.

"I envy you, and Meliantha," she cried, her voice quivering when she spoke.

I sauntered up beside her and watched the tears flow down her cheeks. I'd never really spent much time with her before, but being so close to her made it feel as if she was truly my sister. It was a feeling I'd never had before growing up with only brothers. Calista was always so strong, but anyone could see that she still held the pain in her heart of her lost guardian.

Knowing she needed the comfort, I wrapped my arm around her waist and let her lay her head on my shoulder. "I'm sorry, Calista. I don't know what I'd do without Oren. I know it's a great sadness you bear on your heart."

She shrugged half-heartedly. "It's just hard sometimes when I see all of you with your guardians, it reminds me of what I lost. I can feel Merrick's essence inside me, giving me strength, but I still miss seeing his smiling face. He was my best friend."

While listening to Calista talk, I had an idea form in my head. I wasn't too sure how far my capabilities could go or what kind of limit I was bound to, but what I had in mind was definitely worth a try.

"Calista, look at me," I said, circling around to face her. She sniffed and took a deep breath before lifting her gaze. Her tear-streaked cheeks were flushed, but she gave me a half- smile anyway. I asked her, "What would you do if you could see

Merrick again?"

"What wouldn't I do would be the question. First, I'd thank the heavens and the stars for allowing me that honor, and second, I'd tell him how much I missed him."

I nodded, swallowing hard and trying not to cry from her pain. I would've done anything to see Oren if the situation was turned.

"Why did you ask me that?" she asked.

I paused, then softly said, "Because I think I know a way you can see him again. I never thought about it before until now, but with my dream walking abilities I can try to find him."

Calista fell into the seat behind her while the tears flooded like rivers down her cheeks. "Are you really saying I can see him again?"

I knelt down in front of her, taking her hands in mine. "Yes, Calista. I'm pretty sure I can find him. Would you want to try tonight?"

She squealed and flung her arms around me so tight I could barely breathe. "Yes!" she exclaimed happily. "I would be forever in your debt if you could grant me this."

I laughed, but then struggled to breathe from her excited grip. "Let's just say it's a belated wedding gift to you and my brother. How about that?"

"That sounds perfect." She let me go and hastily wiped the tears from under her eyes while I sucked in a deep breath. "Oh, Sorcha, I'm so sorry. I guess I got a little too excited."

"It's okay." I laughed. "I know how exciting this has to be for you."

"You have no idea. Now let's get you to the throne room. I know everyone's dying to see you, especially your parents."

I strolled alongside her until we got halfway down the corridor. "Wait, I forgot something! I'm going to run back and get it from my room, and I'll be down there in just a second."

She grinned and squeezed my hand. "Okay, I'll let them know."

Back in mine and Drake's room, I found what I was searching for, and quickly made my way to the throne room. I could hear everyone speaking to each other as I sauntered up to the door. Once I opened it and came into view, everyone went silent. However, it didn't take my mother long to break that silence.

My mother, Queen Mab, rushed over to me and took my hands. "Oh, my heavens! You don't even look like the same girl anymore," she cried.

"It's because I'm not, Mother."

She waved her hand flippantly in the air. "Oh I know, just don't let the Bitch Queen taint you. After all, you'll be spending more time around her than me now that you're here with all the sun and heat. I just don't see how anyone can stand it."

"Most of us aren't made of ice," Queen Tatiana interrupted with a sneer. "It's just a shame you don't melt." When my mother opened her mouth to make a snide comment, I cut between them and held up my hands.

"Stop!" I commanded forcefully, glaring at them both. All eyes pivoted to the altercation with curiosity, but I didn't care. "Can you for once play nice with each other? I don't know why you two are like this, but it's got to stop. Look around you … look at our beautiful families. It's growing and becoming stronger. Put your differences aside and keep it that way until we defeat the dark sorcerer. You can always go back to your bitching after that. Can you do that, for everyone's sake?"

It was a bold move, but someone needed to step up and say something. Surprisingly, it was Queen Tatiana that folded. She placed her golden skinned hand on my shoulder and squeezed. "You're right, Sorcha. This is a wonderful day, and I don't want to spoil it for you. It brings me joy to see my son so happy. We're family now, so if you ever need anything you know you can come to me."

I smiled, and placed a hand over hers. "Thank you."

She beamed lovingly at me, but then threw an icy glare at my mother before marching her way over to Meliantha and the twins. My mother agreed to the temporary truce, earning a grin from me in return even though it took great effort for her to agree.

Oren caught my eye, and called me over. I left

my mother and greeted him with a warm embrace. He whispered in my ear, "You're hiding something, *ai dulin*. I can feel it. What's got you so excited that you can't tell me?"

I snickered, and whispered back, "I can't tell you, but you'll find out soon."

I kissed him on the cheek, and moved to my father, who crushed me in a bear hug.

"I'm so glad you're all right," my father sighed. "We came to the Summer Court the moment we found out what happened."

"I'm okay. You know I can handle myself."

"That's for damn sure." He laughed. "Don't be mad, but I already gave Drake the fatherly lecture."

Annoyed, I pulled out of his grasp. "What did you say?"

He shrugged. "Nothing much really, just that if he hurt you I'd come kill him."

Shaking my head, I chuckled. "If he hurt me, I'd kill him."

He kissed me on the forehead. "That's my girl."

Meliantha spotted me and waved me over to her and Kalen where they were both holding onto the babies. I kissed the little ones on the cheeks, and noticed my brother gawking at me with a smirk on his face. "What is it, Kalen?"

"I was just thinking about something. When you and Drake have babies, will they come out looking like dragons?" he joked.

"Um … I hope not, and anyway, I don't see myself as the domesticated type yet." One day I would love to have kids, but I knew I wasn't ready for them yet. Drake and I had too many adventures to explore.

Meliantha giggled. "You say that now, but I'm sure things will change. You're in luck, though; I don't see Drake being the domesticated type either. Congratulations, by the way, and I'm glad you made it home safely."

I gave her a sideways hug since her daughter was bundled in her arms. "Thank you, and I'm glad I did, too."

My eyes then found Ariella and Brayden who were both on opposite sides of the room. I felt sorry for Ariella because even though she was smiling and playing with little Merrick, I knew she had to be upset over my brother obviously steering clear of her. He had to feel the connection, but being how he's always been, Brayden was the only man in my family that found love as a weakness. Yes, he had women every now and again, but he kept them a secret when he did. I just happened to always catch them leaving his place in the middle of the night. I hoped Ariella could melt that heart of his before she killed him, but the chances were slim of that giving the death stare she gave him across the room. Hopefully, they both would come to their senses.

Once I acknowledged everyone, I finally ambled

over to Drake, whose heated gaze had me melting. He pulled me over by the arm and pressed his lips firmly to mine. "Watching you yell at our mothers was priceless. I think everyone's jaws dropped when you did that."

"I don't know why I did it, it just came out and I kept going with it."

Drake draped his arm around my shoulder. "Well, you did great with them. So how about we get this meeting started?"

I nodded, eager to get it going. "Sounds like a plan to me."

Drake glided to the middle of the room and spoke, grabbing the audience's attention. "Thank you all for coming. So many things have happened over the past couple of days, and I knew we needed to discuss them in private. We don't know who to trust, so for now, anything important needs to be discussed with only us."

Nods and murmurs of agreement filled the room. Drake continued once he had the approval from the room, "You all know about Alston already, and that he was the one who took Sorcha with the dark sorcerer's help. Ariella is the next one on his target, so we need to make sure she's well protected. I know more will be discussed once we plan her Guardian Ceremony. However, something happened last night with Sorcha that concerns us all. The dark sorcerer came to her in her dreams."

The room crackled with dangerous energy as soon as the dark sorcerer was mentioned. Drake eyed me and nodded toward our families, signaling it was my turn to talk about the dream. I joined Drake in the middle of the room and explained, "When the dark sorcerer got my power, he must've acquired my ability to dream walk. Basically, he wanted me to pass along a message to everyone. He has a mortal army ready to fight, and with that mortal army will come a slew of iron weapons, and we all know what that can do to us. He also said he's hidden the scroll where no on other than he knows where to find it."

Calista stepped forward. "How are we going to defeat him if we don't know how? We all know our guardian weapons can hurt him, but that's it, they don't kill him. The scroll was our only hope. There has to be some kind of spell that could lead us to it." She turned and addressed Elvena, "Surely there's something, right?"

Elvena had her eyes trained on me with a sly grin on her face. She answered Calista, but kept her gaze pinpointed on me. "I'm not aware of a spell to do that, child. Although, for some reason I suspect the new Summer Queen has something up her sleeve, and I mean that literally."

Frozen, I stared at her in shock, my heart pounding in my chest. How did she know that? Drake leaned over and whispered in my ear, "What is she talking about?"

L.P. DOVER

Elvena smiled and waved her hand in the air, impatiently. "We're waiting, child. You weren't planning on keeping everyone in the dark now were you?"

"How did you know?" I asked her, stuttering in disbelief.

"I could sense it the moment you walked in the room."

Drake furrowed his brows in confusion. "Have you been keeping secrets from me?"

"Yes, but I wanted it to be a surprise for when we were all together." I laughed and slowly pulled the hidden object from underneath my sleeve and held it in the air. Gasps reverberated through the room, along with cheers of excitement. They all knew what it was.

Delighted, Drake asked, "Is that what I think it is?"

I kissed him on the lips. "Yes!"

I carefully handed it to Elvena who held it in her hands and gawked at it for the longest time. If anyone knew how to read it clearly it'd be her. It was written in the Old Fae language.

"How is this possible?" Drake questioned. "I saw you give it to the sorcerer."

"Oh, I did give a scroll to the dark sorcerer, but it wasn't the right one." I spoke the last part while glancing at Oren, wondering if he'd catch on.

He narrowed his eyes, contemplating my meaning, and when he realized what I did he burst out

250

laughing. "Are you saying he has your letter instead of the scroll?"

I nodded cheerfully. "That's exactly what I'm saying. I guess being pissed at Drake paid off."

"Hey!" Drake interceded. "Do you mind explaining? I would sure like to know."

Taking a deep breath, I let it all out with a sigh. I kept my gaze on Drake when I answered, "Okay, here it goes. When I went to the Spring Court to visit Meliantha, Kalen, and the babies, I was so mad at you for being distant with me. I didn't expect you to think our dreams were real, but after the dream where you told me to stay away from you I got angry. I was mad, so I wrote a letter to you. The morning I was going to give it to you, you had already left. I kept it and put it in my pouch on my armor belt. When I got the scroll, I put it in there as well. Then when the sorcerer came and demanded it, I carefully felt around and picked the letter in hopes he wouldn't notice. Thankfully, he didn't look at it before he hid it again."

The room exploded into cheers and laughter after the good news was spilled. Drake picked me up and swung me around in his arms. "You're amazing, you know that?"

"Oh, I know," I agreed teasingly. "We have the advantage now. He has no idea we have the scroll, which means we're going to surprise the hell out of him when we defeat him."

He set me down, and pierced me with a serious

glare. "Although, I think I'm kind of pissed you didn't tell me you had the scroll."

I grinned. "A girl has to be able to have some secrets."

"Good luck, Drake. My little sister is sneaky," Kalen piped in, joining us. "She was always the sly one in our family."

I scowled at him half-heartedly. "No, I think that would be you. Everything I've learned has been from you and Ryder, but all of my underhanded tactics was because of *you*, Kalen. I guess, in this case, taking after you came in handy."

He chuckled lightly. "I'm glad I could help."

The conversations ceased the moment Elvena came into view. She strutted her way to the middle of the room with the open scroll in her hands. She went first to Calista and grabbed her hand, pulling her toward Meliantha where she linked their hands together. Elvena then motioned for me to hold Meliantha's other hand while Ariella joined in with mine and Calista's. The moment the circle was complete, a surge of raw power flowed through us, taking our breath away.

"Do you feel it?" Elvena asked, walking around our circle. From our gasps and wide eyes she knew very well we felt it, so she continued with her speech, "What you feel is all your power connecting and strengthening off each other. It's not at its prime yet, but it will be when Ariella comes into her full power.

Imagine how strong you're going to be then."

Ariella was the one who spoke up. "What's going to happen when I get my full power? What does the scroll say we have to do?"

Elvena reluctantly met our gazes one by one, and it was perfectly clear that she was keeping something from us, something grim, but it didn't seem like she wanted to discuss it in the filled room. Whatever was written in the scroll wasn't going to be easy, that was for sure. I just wondered what it was. Holding up the scroll, Elvena addressed the room, her soft, angelic voice echoing off the walls.

"To defeat the dark sorcerer we need the blood of the Four ... the bonded blood of the Four. Which means Ariella will need to be bonded to Brayden for this to work." Ariella groaned and met Brayden's gaze across the room where he stood unmoving beside my father, King Madoc. Her groan elicited no reaction from him, which only made her fume even more. It was looking like Brayden was going to need some sense smacked into him after this meeting.

I squeezed Ariella's hand to give her reassurance, and she sighed before squeezing mine back. I leaned into her and whispered softly, "It's going to be okay. Brayden isn't the type to express his feelings, and neither am I really, but Drake has helped with that. I know he's feeling the connection, but he probably just needs more time to process everything. He'll come around."

"I guess we'll see," she whispered, gritting her teeth. Brayden's gaze was lowered to the floor, and I was sure he'd balk at the sight of Ariella staring daggers at him. Her icy and violent stare would make any Winter Fae cower away from her. She was going to do great in the Winter Court.

"Does it say why the blood has to be bonded?" Ariella asked. "My blood should still be the same, bonded or not."

Elvena shook her head. "No, my child, it won't. Right now we have Calista with Fall blood, Meliantha with Spring, Sorcha with Summer, and you. As of right now you're Summer, but we need you to be the Winter."

Ariella clenched her jaw and lowered her head. "Thank you. Unfortunately, I get it now." She released mine and Calista's hand and stepped back. The strong flow of magic was gone with her absence. "If you'll excuse me, I need to get some fresh air."

She hastily retreated out of the room, keeping her gaze on the door while Brayden finally showed the first real emotion the whole time he'd been there. Worry crossed his face, but once she was out of the room the blank mask fell into place. He really needed his ass kicked.

To get the focus off Ariella's departure, I decided to speak up. "How is our blood going to defeat the dark sorcerer?"

Elvena explained, "We need to have a special

weapon made, preferably by Durin since he's the most powerful of the dwarves. Each of you will go through the process of letting this weapon take your blood, the same way you do it in the Guardian ceremonies. Once the blood has been taken, the weapon will be indestructible and the sole key in killing the dark sorcerer. When it pierces his blackened heart it'll be all over. Every bit of power he took will be restored back into the land. The Black Forest will be no more … he will be no more."

The room went quiet, especially since Ariella stormed out, and it was hard to get excited about defeating the dark sorcerer when the couple we needed to complete the bond didn't look like they were going to be bonded anytime soon. However, Elvena hadn't explained everything, and I had a feeling she didn't want us all to know.

When everyone left to celebrate, Calista, Meliantha, and I stayed behind to question Elvena. "What aren't you telling us?" Calista demanded. "You may be able to fool everyone else, but you can't fool me."

Elvena sighed and hung her head. "It's not something to worry about right now. There's still plenty of time ahead of us until we can even think about making the weapon, since the current state of Ariella and Brayden's union is complicated."

Her grim expression didn't imply there wasn't anything to worry about. I wanted to know, and I *was* going to find out. I snapped at her, "I saw your face, Elvena, and it sure as hell appeared to be a look that it was something we needed to worry about. If I have to take the scroll away from you and decipher it myself I will."

"All right, child, I'll tell you," Elvena whispered regretfully.

"Do I need to fetch Ariella?" Meliantha asked, cutting in.

Elvena's eyes went wide. "No! I don't want her in here. She has so much to worry about right now. I can't put this burden on her."

"Did the scroll mention something having to do with Ariella?" I questioned curiously.

"That's the thing," Elvena whispered sadly. "You all have sacrificed so much, and now one of you might have to sacrifice it all. If what the scroll says is true, I fear it's going to have to be Ariella that kills him, and I just don't know what the outcome of that will be."

We all stiffened as the realization of what she said sunk in. Meliantha shook her head forcefully and paced the room. "Please don't tell me she's going to die if she kills that son of a bitch. You're not saying that, right?"

Elvena staggered to a nearby chair and sat down, looking ancient and defeated. "To be honest, I'm not sure. The scroll states that the only one with the ability to kill the dark sorcerer will be the one who can earn his trust. We all know he's not going to trust any of you, which leaves only one left. Since Ariella hasn't fully come into her power, we need to wait and see what happens before we tell her. I don't want her knowing yet. We'll cross that bridge when the time comes."

My mind reeled with the fact that out of the four of us, it was going to all come down to the one that I'd least expected. "How is she going to earn his trust? I don't like the way this sounds," I admitted forlornly.

I didn't want to think about it, much less tell Drake what was going on. Elvena sobbed, "I'm sorry you all had to find out like this. I worry about how Ariella will take it once she finds out."

Calista knelt down and held Elvena's hands. "Once she comes into her power and bonds with Brayden we'll figure it out. For now, we need to live our lives and enjoy every minute of it. We have plenty of time to come up with other options, but until then we speak of this to no one. I'm not going to let anything happen to my family, especially Ariella." She extended her hand and held it out to us. "I say we make our own destiny. Are you with me?"

I placed my hand on top of hers. "I'm with you, no matter what I have to do to keep everyone safe."

Meliantha followed and slapped her hand on top of mine. "That bastard isn't going to touch Ariella. I'll hunt him down to the end of time if I have to. I'm with you, always."

Our silent agreement was going to be hard to keep from Drake, but I knew it had to be done. We had no clue what was going to happen with Ariella and Brayden, but until they bonded there was nothing we *could* do, but sit and wait.

Epilogue

Sorcha

"Why ... must ... you ... torture ... me?" Drake asked while trailing kisses down my neck to my collarbone.

Moaning, I tilted my head back in the water. "Because I can," I taunted back.

The current of the water rocked us back and forth, already fueling our hunger for each other by making our bodies move together in a tantalizing rhythm. We spent the night in our underwater retreat, and instead of getting dressed we decided to spend the day in the water, exploring its depths.

"Well, since you abandoned me in the dream realm, again for the second night in a row, I have to make up for all the time we missed." Wrapped around his body, he was already hard between my legs. It was sublime being able to spend every waking hour with him and no distractions. It would soon come to a close once things were set in motion.

He lifted my chin gently with his hand. "What's

wrong, beautiful? You seem distracted. Did something happen in your dream that you aren't telling me?"

My throat tightened up at the remembrance of my dream. I witnessed the most heart wrenching sight of my life, and I'd never forget the look on Calista's face for as long as I lived when she saw Merrick for the first time. "I was with Calista last night, Drake. I did something that I didn't think I could do, but it worked. I found Merrick in the Hereafter and linked him to the dream I was sharing with Calista."

Drake's mouth flew open. "You did that? I didn't know you could talk to people in the Hereafter. How did it go?"

I smiled, and a tear escaped the corner of my eye. "You know I'm not the type of person to cry over sentimental matters, but seeing them together was one of the most beautiful things I'd ever seen."

Drake took my face in his hands and kissed me deeply. "You're the most beautiful thing I've ever seen. I love you, Sorcha. How about we make love right here, right now, for the rest of the night. Then, tomorrow I can teach you how to transform into your dragon?"

Nodding, I plastered a smile onto my face even though I was nervous about transforming into my dragon. Drake, however, put my mind at ease by devouring my body to near exhaustion. The night ended, giving me the best night's sleep I'd had in a long time.

Collapsing onto the sand, sweaty and exhausted, I had my first transformation into the dragon. "You were amazing up there," Drake uttered whole-heartedly. "I can't believe how fast a flyer you are, and what's even greater is that you're a frost breathing dragon. I guess your Winter side didn't want to let you go."

I snorted. "I guess not, but opposites attract right? My frost to your flame …"

Drake smiled down at me. "I like the sound of that. Okay, beautiful, we have two weeks until we're needed at Ariella's Guardian Ceremony. What new adventures do you want to go on in the meantime?"

Wrapping my arms around his neck, I tugged him down closer to me. "Anything with you is an adventure, but preferably I'd love to stay with you here, just like this."

Balancing on his arms, he rose above me and stared lovingly in my eyes. "I think I can handle that, but the question is … can you?"

With a wicked grin, I ran my hands down his

chest. "I guess you'll have to find out."

There was so much on my mind, but for the time being I let it all slip away while I relished in the joys of our court and our time together. The end was near, I could feel it, and so could the land. I had to believe we would win, to defeat the evil once and for all, and come out stronger. The energy of my court crackled underneath my fingertips as I delved them into the sand. This was my home and my land, and I had to protect it. It was mine and Drake's Summer ... our Summer of Frost.

The End

Read on to find out what happened in Calista and Merrick's dream.

Calista and Merrick's Dream

Calista

"Are you sure you want to do this?" Ryder asked softly, tucking a strand of hair behind my ear. We were lying in bed, snuggled together with his arm around my waist, holding me tight.

Slowly, I turned my head to face him and whispered, "More than anything."

He gently caressed my arm, moving up and down in calming motions. I wanted sleep to come, but I was too anxious, and scared that Sorcha wouldn't be able to bring Merrick to the dream. I tried not to get excited about it just in case it didn't work, but my heart betrayed me and filled me with hope.

"What if Sorcha can't find Merrick? Will you be okay with that?"

I shrugged noncommittally. "I'm not going to lie, it'll hurt, but if I could just talk to him and make sure he's okay I'll be happy. His absence will always be there, but the pain will be less. After all these years I still feel it as if it happened yesterday."

Ryder sighed and tucked me under his arm, where I lay my head on his chest. He rubbed my back as I curled into him, trailing my fingers over the deep ridges of his stomach. His heart beat steadily under my ear, a continuous rhythm that brought comfort and joy to my life. He was mine and he loved me, but he wouldn't be here if it wasn't for my fallen guardian, Merrick. Merrick saved Ryder's life and paid the ultimate price, but he did it for me because he loved me and knew that my life would be empty without Ryder.

Taking deep, calming breaths, I closed my eyes and willed sleep to come. Ryder kissed my forehead and continued his slow, soft caresses up and down my back. "That's it, my love. Go to sleep ..."

The sounds began to fade, and my body felt like it was floating away as I was pulled from my mind to another place, the dream realm.

Sorcha was waiting for me, holding out her hand, with a smile on her face. Anxiously, I took her hand, looking around nervously.

"He's not here yet," Sorcha informed me.

"Oh," I replied half-heartedly, looking away.

She squeezed my hand and smiled. "I wanted to ask you if there's a place you'd like me to take you, and to also get you to take that look of disappointment off your face." When I opened my mouth to speak, she cut me off. "There's no need to explain, I understand. This is a big deal for you, but you need to stop doubting me. I'll get him here. Tell me … do you two have a special place, a place where you and Merrick share happy memories?"

Nodding, I bit my lip to distract myself from the tears that threatened to spill at any moment. "Yes," I answered softly. "There's a field we played in as children. It's also the place where he secretly trained me, and where his ashes are scattered."

"I would say that is a special place, indeed." Sorcha approached me and placed her hands on both sides of my head. "Okay, here's what I want you to do. I want you to close your eyes and picture this field in your mind; the smells, the air, the wind as it blows through the trees. I want you to be there, body and soul, and hold onto it."

Closing my eyes, I did as she said. The field came easily to my mind, as did the memories of my time there with Merrick. The air was thick and humid, hot from the Summer sun, but the smells were what reminded me of my old home. The smell of honeysuckle and fresh green grass filled my senses, bringing a smile to my face. I could feel it all around me.

Sorcha sighed and let go of my head. "Open your eyes, Calista. It's beautiful."

The moment my eyes opened I couldn't hold the tears back any longer. "This is it," I breathed. "Now what do we do?"

Smiling, Sorcha slowly began to walk away. Her lower lip quivered when she spoke, "Right now I'm going to leave you, Calista."

Confused, I started toward her, not understanding why she was leaving me. Could she not bring Merrick? The sound of someone calling my name behind me rooted me to the ground.

"Cali?"

My heart stopped beating, and my breath came out as rapid pants, making me feel lightheaded. "I imagined his voice," I whispered to myself. "Yes, it was just my imagination."

"Well, I see you're still as stubborn as ever. I guess nothing's changed in the last five years." When I didn't turn around, he huffed out an exasperated breath. His voice, his humorous tone, was just like Merrick. "If you don't turn I'm going to make you, and you know how I loved throwing you around so you could kick my ass."

It was him!

Turning around quickly, I frantically raked my eyes over my guardian standing before me. "Please tell me this is real," I choked out, sobbing.

Merrick opened his arms and laughed. "Get your ass over here, Cali!"

Not wasting a second, I ran and flung myself into his arms, crying the whole way. "Merrick, I've missed you so much! There are so many things that have happened over the years, and I'd give anything to have you there with me."

As I held him, I breathed him in deeply, remembering how it used to give me comfort growing up. He was my best friend and he was always there, taking care of me.

"I know," he whispered, releasing his hold so he could look at my face. "I've missed you, too. I've been watching over you this whole time. It appears even in death we're still connected."

His brown eyes were still the same—all warm and loving—and his hair was still the same bright blond that slightly curled around the edges of his face. He hadn't changed a bit. Lifting my hands, I traced the planes of his face, and ran them through his golden locks like I used to do when we were together.

"So you know everything?" I asked softly.

"Yes, Cali, I know everything. I was there when the land crowned you Fall Queen, and I was here in this field when you came to talk to me, even though you thought I wasn't there. I was there when Sorcha told you she could bring me here, so needless to say, I was expecting you."

The tears streamed down my face, and he gently wiped them away with the pad of his thumbs. Taking my chin in his hand, he lifted up my face and smiled down at me. "Out of everything I've seen you accomplish and do to make our land better, nothing

*will ever compare to the day you gave birth to your
son. The way your face looked and the smile you gave
him when you named him after me. That has stayed
with me and given me joy."*

*"I never knew you were there with me," I
confessed sheepishly.*

*"Yes, you did. You just didn't realize I was
actually there. You said it yourself, you could feel me
inside your heart. Now think back to every time you
had to clutch your chest from your heart fluttering out
of control. How many times did it feel so full of love
that you thought it would burst? That was me,
Calista. That was you feeling my happiness and
love."*

*I was so scared to ask him my next question, but I
had to know. "Merrick," I began. "Are you happy in
the Hereafter?"*

*He laughed, and the familiar rumble in his chest
made my heart feel lighter. "Of course, I'm happy.
Yes, I miss you, and I would give anything to be there
with you and meet your son, but I'm where I'm
supposed to be."*

*"Will you always be with me? Are you always
going to be there even though I can't see you?"*

*"For the most part, yes, but mainly in the times
you really need me or wish me there. I can feel the
tug on my soul when you need me, and it pulls me to
you. I've seen you sad so many times, and I prayed
that you'd be able to hear me just once so I could*

beat some sense into you."

I laughed because I could just picture him yelling at me to stop my blubbering. Merrick laughed along with me, but then stopped and shook his head. Taking my face with both hands, he kissed me on the cheek. "I hate seeing you sad, Calista. Just always know that I'm there with you. In here ..." he said, placing his hand over my heart, the same way he did when he was dying all those years ago.

I placed my hand over his, and squeezed. Sorcha caught my attention as she made her way swiftly to us. She acknowledged Merrick with a nod of her head before saying, "I can feel the dream starting to shudder. We're almost out of time. I just wanted you to know so you could say your good-byes."

When she turned to leave, Merrick called out. "Wait! Is there any way for you to do this again someday?"

Sorcha turned her head and winked. "I'm sure it can be arranged."

Merrick and I both howled in delight as he picked me up and twirled me around the field. "You see, Cali. I'll never leave you. There will never be a good-bye."

"Never," I repeated jubilantly.

In the next moment, the dream world started to shift and fade. Merrick pulled me in quickly and held me close, not letting go. Quickly he said, "I'm not going to say farewell to you because I know I'll see you again. Just remember, I'm always there when you need me."

"I won't forget," I whispered, crying softly. Tilting my head back, I stared into his soft, brown eyes. "I love you, Merrick, my guardian."

He placed his hand on my cheek and sighed. "I know."

Those hushed words were the last ones I heard before everything faded away and I was thrust out of the dream realm with more love in my heart, and happiness in my soul.

Acknowledgments

To my husband—Thank you for your love and understanding of my passion. Some days I know it's not easy to deal with me, but you do knowing that I'm doing what I love. You will always and forever be my rock, the one thing that holds me steady.

To my crazy friends—Jenna Pizzi, Amber Garcia, Jimie, Francesca, Sarah Davey, Shanora, Desiree, Kathryn, Jessie, Cassie, Derinda, and so many more—I appreciate you always being there for me and constantly helping me out when I am in need. I couldn't have asked for anything better. I love you all.

To my Guardian team—I want to thank you so much for all your hard work and devotion. You all are the best!

To the Indie Inked group—What can I say? You ladies are amazing! I never knew how tight knit a group of authors could be until I was asked to join in with you. You all are my family, and your guidance and support has been phenomenal. I look forward to watching our group flourish and thrive over the years.

To Regina—I love you and your amazing work that you've done for me and my books. I will treasure my covers for the rest of my life. You are one talented woman, and your future is going to be as bright as the brightest star.

To Melissa—You are the most amazing editor in the world.

To Julie—Thank you for making my books beautiful on the inside with your amazing talent.

To my beloved fans—I would be nowhere without you. I want to thank you all for taking a chance on me and finding joy in my books. I will always and forever be grateful to you. I hope to always be able to give you books you can enjoy and cherish.

About the Author

L.P. Dover lives in the beautiful state of North Carolina with her husband and two wonderful daughters. She's an avid reader that loves her collection of books. Writing has always been her passion and she's delighted to share it with the world. L.P. Dover spent several years in college starting out with a major in Psychology and then switching to dental. She worked in the dental field for eight years and then decided to stay home with her two beautiful girls. She spent the beginning of her reading years indulging in suspense thrillers, but now she can't get away from the paranormal/fantasy books. Now that she has started on her passion and began writing, you won't see her go anywhere without a notebook, pen, and her secret energy builder…chocolate.

For more information about L.P. Dover and her books, visit:

Facebook/L.P. Dover
https://www.facebook.com/pages/LP-Dover/318455714919114?fref=ts

Website/Blog
http://authorlpdoverbooks.com/

Goodreads
http://www.goodreads.com/author/show/6526309.L_P_Dover

Twitter
https://twitter.com/LPDover

Other Works by L.P. Dover

The FOREVER FAE Series
Forever Fae & Betrayals of Spring

The SECOND CHANCES Series
Love's Second Chance

Also Check Out These Extraordinary Authors & Books:

Alivia Anders ~ Illumine
Cambria Hebert ~ Recalled
Angela Orlowski Peart ~ Forged by Greed
Julia Crane ~ Freak of Nature
J. A. Huss ~ Clutch
Cameo Renae ~ Hidden Wings
Alexia Purdy ~ Reign of Blood
Tabatha Vargo ~ On the Plus Side
Beth Balmanno ~ Set in Stone
Lizzy Ford ~ Dark Summer (Witchling Saga #1)
Ella James ~ Selling Scarlett
Tara West ~ Visions of the Witch
Heidi McLaughlin ~ Forever Your Girl
Melissa Andrea ~ Flutter
Komal Lewis ~ Falling for Hadie
Melissa Pearl ~ Betwixt
Sarah M. Ross ~ Awaken
Brina Courtney ~ Reveal

34527070R00170

Made in the USA
Lexington, KY
11 August 2014